Suddenly, with a great surge of loneliness, Mike pictured his mother and father and his brothers and sisters in the small room they had once shared in New York City before Da had died, before Mike had been arrested as a copper stealer. Mike had only been trying to help feed his family—he'd never expected his theft to divide the Kellys.

If only the earning of money just for food and a place to live hadn't been so hard, Mike thought. *If only Da hadn't died.*

"Da," Mike whispered, as he pictured his father's kind face. "Oh, Da, what should I do? What would you have me do?"

He held his breath, hoping for an answer, but all he heard was the rat-a-tat of an imaginary drum.

I know the drum calls, Mike told himself, *and that's what counts, because Jeb says the army badly needs drummers.*

As he listened to the bugle's call and saw the flag held high, he burned with eagerness. He had to join the army! He had to!

ALSO AVAILABLE BY JOAN LOWERY NIXON IN LAUREL-LEAF BOOKS:

LAND OF DREAMS

LAND OF HOPE

LAND OF PROMISE

A FAMILY APART

CAUGHT IN THE ACT

IN THE FACE OF DANGER

A PLACE TO BELONG

KEEPING SECRETS

CIRCLE OF LOVE

A Dangerous Promise

Joan Lowery Nixon

Published by
Bantam Doubleday Dell Books for Young Readers
a division of
Bantam Doubleday Dell Publishing Group, Inc.
1540 Broadway
New York, New York 10036

ISBN: 0-440-21965-5

RL: 5.8

Reprinted by arrangement with Delacorte Press

Printed in the United States of America

January 1996

10

OPM

With grateful thanks to
Mary Ellen Johnson
who founded the
Orphan Train Heritage Society of America
in order to honor the orphan train riders
and preserve their history.

A Note from the Author

During the years from 1854 to 1929, the Children's Aid Society, founded by Charles Loring Brace, sent more than 100,000 children on orphan trains from the slums of New York City to new homes in the West. This placing-out program was so successful that other groups, such as the New York Foundling Hospital, followed the example.

The Orphan Train Adventures were inspired by the true stories of these children; but the characters in the series, their adventures, and the dates of their arrival are entirely fictional. We chose St. Joseph, Missouri, between the years 1860 and 1880 as our setting in order to place our characters in one of the most exciting periods of American history. As for the historical figures who enter these stories—they very well could have been at the places described at the proper times, to touch the lives of the children who came west on the orphan trains.

Joan Lowery Nixon

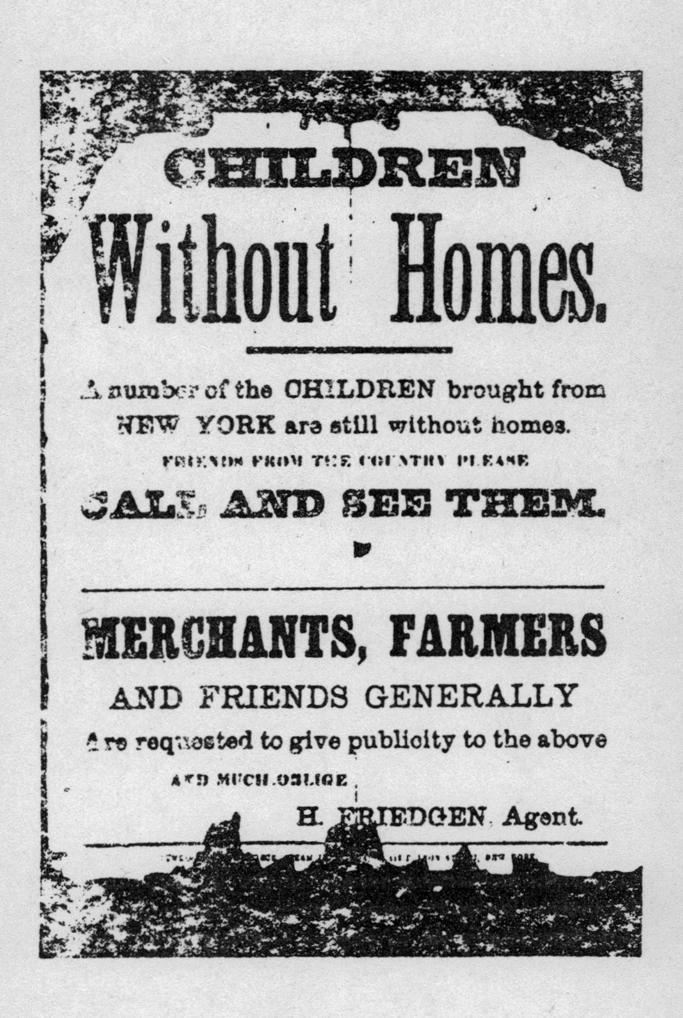
CHILDREN
Without Homes.
A number of the CHILDREN brought from NEW YORK are still without homes.
FRIENDS FROM THE COUNTRY PLEASE
CALL AND SEE THEM.
MERCHANTS, FARMERS
AND FRIENDS GENERALLY
Are requested to give publicity to the above
AND MUCH OBLIGE
H. FRIEDGEN, Agent.

1

"GRANDMA, WILL YOU read us another story from Frances Mary's journal? Now? Right now?" Jeff Collins begged as he pushed his chair back from the breakfast table.

Jennifer Collins scowled at her twelve-year-old brother. "*After* we do the dishes," Jennifer reminded him, glad that it was his turn to clean the kitchen and not hers.

"That's right," Grandma said, and smiled at Jennifer. "After dishes, *and* after beds have been made."

"Ooops!" Jennifer said, and scrambled out of her chair, heading for the stairs. She should have remembered to make her bed and pick up the clothes she'd scattered around her room. Grandma's house would be their home until the end of summer, when Dad would return from his overseas assignment and they'd learn where the family would be transferred.

Jennifer remembered her early reluctance at spending what she was sure would be a boring summer in Grandma's small Missouri town while Mom secluded herself in an upstairs bedroom in order to write a novel.

How wrong she had been!

Ever since Grandma had brought out the journal written by Jennifer's great-great-great-grandmother, Frances Mary Kelly, Jennifer couldn't learn enough about the Kelly family, who had come to St. Joseph, Missouri, in 1860, on one of the orphan trains from New York City.

Thinking about the stories that were to come, Jennifer and Jeff sped through their chores. Soon they were seated in the wicker furniture on the screened porch, while Grandma settled into the rocker opposite them with Frances Mary's journal open on her lap.

Grandma began to read.

We knew war was coming. There was no way to escape it. Even before Abraham Lincoln's inauguration as President of the United States on March 4, 1861, the southern states had begun seceding from the Union; so while we rejoiced that Kansas was granted statehood and admitted to the Union on January 29, we could not forget our fear of what might happen to a country so bitterly divided.

In February all our fears became realities. Representatives from the southern states met in Montgomery, Alabama, and adopted a constitution for a Confederate government. The Confederacy even inaugurated its own president, Jefferson Davis. With the formation of a separate rebellious government, we gave up any hope of solving the slavery issue peacefully. It would be North against South, neighbor against neighbor, and we were all fearful.

I confess that I carried an extra worry within my heart. I knew my brother Mike, loyal, brave, and impulsive, wouldn't be content to remain at home with his foster mother, Mrs. Taylor, when the activity of war beckoned all around him—especially since Captain Taylor, his foster father, would be leading his own company into battle.

After the first shot was fired upon Fort Sumter on April 12, Mike proved that I was right about him. In his subsequent letter Mike wrote with excitement about volunteers being trained and plans being made at Fort Leavenworth. Did Mike wish to participate in these plans? I hurried to write and remind him that war was not an exciting adventure, it was horrible. I pointed out that men must be at least sixteen in order to serve as soldiers, and he was only a boy of twelve.

"Twelve, but close to thirteen," Mike finally replied. "And I've grown an inch or more since you last saw me. Captain Taylor and his company left by train for Virginia to join Brigadier General McDowell's regiments, but Fort Leavenworth's still busier than the New York docks with five ships in port. There's an old feller here named Jebediah—we call him Jeb—and he's taught me all ten drum calls a drummer boy needs to know."

In spite of the warm weather, I shivered as I read his parting words: "You may know what is best for you, Frances Mary, but there's no way you can judge what is best for me. Only I can do that." And then he teased, "Tell me, how can you know anything about war—a gentle (but bossy) girl who's never been near a battlefield?"

2

"MICHAEL?"

Mike Kelly stretched in his chair and gazed out the window to watch a ragtag group of volunteers straggling in uneven formation across the sunbaked Fort Leavenworth parade ground. Their uniforms were just as haphazard, whatever the supply officer could come up with: forage caps, dark blue jackets that didn't fit, and light blue pants—many of them made of shoddy, a cheap wool mixture that fell apart when it got wet.

The men's shoes were an odd assortment of everything from brogans to boots, with a wisp of hay tied to the left foot, a wisp of straw tied to the right. Sergeant Duncan, frustrated that many of the farm boys didn't know their right foot from their left, had changed the marching cadence from "left . . . right" to "hayfoot . . . strawfoot." In spite of the sergeant's efforts, one of the men, seeming to be still confused, tripped and stumbled over the man in front of him, and they both fell to the ground. As a purple-faced Sergeant Duncan ordered a halt, Mike chuckled.

"Michael! Try to keep your mind on your lessons."

Mike turned to face his foster mother, Louisa Taylor, who shook her head at him sadly.

"Granted, you're a quick student and good at both reading and mathematics, but you can't learn what I'm trying to teach you and stare out the window at the same time."

This pretty young woman who sat across the table from him tried her best to look stern, but her eyes began to twinkle, and a smile spread across her face.

Mike grinned in response. "That's a sorry group of soldiers out there on the parade ground," he said. "I can't see how they'll march to battle if they can't stay upright."

Louisa's smile vanished, and her eyes darkened with worry. "If only they didn't have to go to battle," she said. "If only our leaders could have solved the slavery problem peacefully, we wouldn't be at war."

"Those Rebs weren't about to listen to reason," Mike answered, but he broke off. That wasn't what Mrs. Taylor wanted to hear. "Don't worry about the captain, ma'am," Mike said, and reached across the table to touch her hand. "He's a good, well-trained officer. He'll come through this war all right."

Louisa looked at him hopefully. "I thank God that the captain's life was spared during the skirmishes in Virginia. Big Bethel was a sad defeat for our Union Army, but the captain wrote that the men acquitted themselves as well as could be expected, since most were inexperienced volunteers."

Mike shook his head angrily. "The Rebs shouldn't have won a single battle. I wish I'd been there. I'd have helped to change the score!" Mike could visualize himself in the thick of the fight, charging ahead through the smoke and gun blasts. Some of the volunteers had turned and run; Mike would have pressed forward no matter what.

Louisa stretched across the table to tousle Mike's curly red hair. "It's a blessing to all of us that you aren't old enough to be called to fight. You should be safe here at the fort, and if our many prayers are answered, the war will be over soon."

Mike squirmed uncomfortably in his chair. Safe at the fort? Did they think he was a small child, needing protection?

Louisa seemed not to notice Mike's fidgeting. "I enclosed your letter to the captain in the letter I sent to him this morning," she said. "The best thing we can do is to write to him often." Sitting a little straighter in her chair, Louisa picked up Mike's copybook. "Now then, let's get back to the lesson."

But from outside the open window came the ever louder stamp of boots and Sergeant Duncan's booming voice as he counted cadence, and Mike couldn't resist twisting in his chair for one quick look.

"Oh, Mike, Mike," Louisa said with an exaggerated sigh. "All right, run outside and watch. We'll work on your lessons later."

Mike nearly upended his chair in his hurry. "It's exciting —all the comings and goings and bugles and drumbeats and such."

"War is *not* exciting," Louisa told him.

"Ma'am, you sound like my sister, Frances Mary," Mike teased, and he ran outside to the front porch of the officers' quarters, which faced the parade ground. Mike's heartbeat quickened as a flag bearer passed by, and he stood stiffly at attention. *Women don't understand about these things*, he told himself.

For a moment Mike could see himself holding the Union flag high, leading the way as mounted officers and foot soldiers followed him into battle. Cannonballs whizzed past, and gunshots rang in his ears, but Mike bravely pressed on.

The dream of glory was short-lived. Mike was more than

three years shy of the accepted age for becoming a soldier. Sergeant Duncan had laughed when Mike had told him he wanted to enlist.

"Don't try lyin' about your age with me, boyo," the sergeant had said with a whoop of laughter. "We've got plenty of men willing to fight for the Union, so there's been no talk of forming a little kiddies' army as yet."

He'd laughed again, and Mike had stalked away, angry. If the sergeant only knew it, Mike would make a better soldier than any of those raw recruits on the parade ground who were still trying to pick up their feet and put them in the right places without causing disaster.

Todd Blakely, Captain Blakely's son, appeared across the parade ground and waved to Mike, yelling, "Come on! Jeb wants to see us!"

Dodging two sutlers' wagons loaded with supplies for sale and a row of tents that had sprung up sometime during the night, Mike ran around the end of the parade ground to join Todd.

Todd had a shock of thick blond hair and gangly arms and legs. His arms constantly thrust out of sleeves, and his pants legs were always too short, no matter how often his mother let out the hems. Todd had become Mike's best friend at the fort, and it was Todd who two weeks earlier had introduced Mike to Jebediah, the elderly soldier who knew all the drum calls.

Gap-toothed Jebediah, whose limp testified to the two shots he had taken in the Indian wars, had led the boys to a tack room at one end of the stables, which were pungent with the acrid odors of hay and the sweat of horses. There, Mike and Todd sat on a bale of hay, as Jebediah carefully took a large package from a shelf and slowly unwrapped its cloth covering to expose a drum.

"Belonged to a lad of only nineteen who went down with an arrow in his back," Jebediah'd said. "I snatched up his drum and kept the beat goin'. Stuck by my captain and followed his orders to beat *advance* for the men. We won that battle, and I got praised for my actions by my captain. Even though our company later got a new drummer with his own drum, I hung on to this one because I knew it would come into good use someday. It's about time for it to go back into service. The drum sounds the orders to the men to advance or retreat. A company's handicapped if it hasn't got a drummer."

He'd motioned to Todd to stand, then hung the drum strap around Todd's neck, adjusting the strap so that the large drum hung just above Todd's knees. Painted on the side of the drum was a faded eagle with wings outstretched and a Union flag that waved in an imaginary breeze.

Jebediah had produced two drumsticks and suddenly, magically, beat out a rat-a-tat-tat that made Mike's heart jump.

"Here," he said, thrusting the sticks into Todd's hands. "You try it. Hold them like this. No, this a-way."

Todd was quicker, but soon Mike got the feel of the drumsticks and picked up the rhythms. Ever since that day, the two boys had practiced the drumbeats whenever Jebediah had given permission.

Now, as Mike and Todd ran into the stables, Jeb met them. "You boys have been practicin' the calls for a good long while," he told them. "Now, suppose you show me what you can do."

In the tack room Todd performed first. Then it was Mike's turn. He went through all ten calls, from *reveille*, a sharp rapid beat to wake up the soldiers, to *taps*, the solemn slow drumming that meant lights out and bedtime. Jeb had said that *taps* was a call new to this war. Trying not to think too much about the fact that *taps* was also drummed at funerals, Mike beat out the call, making only one mistake . . . well, maybe two or three.

But instead of praising the boys, Jeb grimaced, showing a mouth with more gaps than teeth. "Good thing you've got years of practice ahead of you afore you're old enough to join up," he said to Mike. "Those beats have got to come out smart and sharp enough to inspire the men. Do you think you can lead men into battle with a thud, thud, thud?"

Mike felt himself blush. "I guess I was concentrating too hard on the beat itself. I'll give it another try," he said.

"Maybe by the time you're sixteen, this war will be over," Jeb answered slyly, "and the army won't have much need of drummers."

Mike thought of Sergeant Duncan, who had laughed at his age and his size. "I may be short for being nearly thirteen, but I'll soon start growing fast," he said. "Won't be long before I can pass for at least a year older."

"I'm two years older than Mike and tall for my age," Todd said. "Anybody'd take me for sixteen. Besides, I've got my own bugle and know all the bugle calls. I've been thinking of joining up."

"So you been sayin'." Jeb glanced at Todd from the corners of his eyes. "I been hearin' that some of the companies bein' put together in such a hurry haven't got drummers or buglers and ain't fussy about ages. A boy close to the age to enlist, showin' up at the right place at the right time with a fine drum like this one or a shiny bugle, just might find himself a part of the Union Army."

"Where's this 'right place'?" Todd asked.

"Down south a-ways at Fort Scott, less'n ninety miles or so, they're mobilizin' a lot of foot soldiers, sendin' 'em out nearly as fast as they show up to enlist."

"Ninety miles? That's a long ways to walk," Mike blurted out.

Jeb's lips turned down in a sneer. "No use joinin' the army if you're afraid of a little walkin'. The fightin' never lasts long at a time. It's the walkin' what soldiers do most of." He chuckled. "Don't know if you can make it in just three days' time, but the Second Kansas Infantry, under Colonel Mitchell, will be leavin' Kansas City, headed into southern Missouri."

"Kansas City isn't far!" Mike exclaimed.

Jeb struggled to his feet. "You can stay here and practice," he said. "I gotta tend the horses." But just before he reached the doorway, he turned to face Todd. "I was just a scrap of a youngster when I signed on because my country needed me," he said. "I know how you feel."

Hurt at being ignored by Jeb, Mike waited until Jeb was out of earshot and said, "The Union Army needs *both* of us."

"Maybe not right now," Todd said.

"You've talked about joining."

"I know, and someday I will. But before my father left for Virginia, he told me the best thing I could do was work hard, study, and take care of my mother and sisters."

Mike said, "Captain Taylor told me nearly the same thing. But we're not children. We can help the Union win the war."

"You're serious, aren't you?"

"Yes. I'm serious."

Todd frowned as he thought. "There's not much I can do to take care of my mother," he said. "If you've noticed, the women seem to take care of each other."

Mike nodded. "And because of the orderlies' help, we don't even have many chores."

"So there's not much we're needed for around here."

"You might even say we're in the way." Mike looked at the drum and then at Todd. "Captain Taylor didn't exactly forbid my joining up—at least, he didn't put it in those words. What about your father?"

Todd scrunched up his forehead as if he were trying hard to remember. "When I said I wished I was old enough to join the army, my father told me he just hoped the war would be over before I had to make that decision."

"So he didn't say, 'You can't become a drummer for the Union Army.' "

"No," Todd said. "He didn't."

As excitement began to shine in Todd's eyes, a slight twinge of guilt that had been pestering Mike dissolved.

"I've heard the Rebs are tough fighters," Todd said. "The army needs all the help it can get."

Mike grinned. "Sergeant Duncan said that under fire some of these Union volunteers get scared and run. I'd never run."

"Me neither."

"The army badly needs drummers and buglers. Jeb said so. We know how to beat the calls. It's a real waste if we don't do anything with what we know."

"It's not only a waste. It's like working *against* the Union when we're needed and don't go."

Mike's heart thumped rapidly, and his voice dropped to almost a whisper. "Then what do you say we make our way down to the Second Kansas Infantry in Kansas City and see if they can use us?"

Todd's words came out in a hoarse growl. "You mean run away?"

"Yes," Mike said. "Run away."

3

DURING THE NIGHT Mike wasn't quite so sure. He thrashed back and forth in bed, both tormented and thrilled by the decision he'd made.

The captain wouldn't approve my going.

Who says he wouldn't? He's a career officer. He'll be proud that I want to serve the Union.

He wants me to take care of Louisa.

She's taking care of me. She doesn't need me to take care of her. And as Todd said, the women take care of each other.

If the captain were here, what would he tell me? He's my father now. Captain Taylor was one of the finest, fairest men Mike ever had met, and he wished with all his heart that he truly could hear what the captain had to say.

Suddenly, with a great surge of loneliness, Mike pictured his mother and father and his brothers and sisters in the small room they had once shared in New York City before Da had died, before Mike had been arrested as a copper stealer. Mike had only been trying to help feed his family—he'd never expected his theft to divide the Kellys.

If only the earning of money just for food and a place to live hadn't been so hard, Mike thought. *If only Da hadn't died.*

"Da," Mike whispered, as he pictured his father's kind face. "Oh, Da, what should I do? What would you have me do?"

He held his breath, hoping for an answer, but all he heard was the rat-a-tat of an imaginary drum.

I know the drum calls, Mike told himself, *and that's what counts, because Jeb says the army badly needs drummers.*

As he listened to the bugle's call and saw the flag held high, he burned with eagerness. He had to join the army! He had to!

Early the next morning, Mike sought out Todd, whose pale face and darkly circled eyes showed that he hadn't slept well either.

While the boys hunkered down in the shade between two of the buildings in the officers' quarters, Todd pulled his pocket watch out of his jacket, fingered it, and shoved it back. Out and back, out and back. Finally, he mumbled, "I've been thinking . . ."

Mike's throat tightened as he waited for Todd to go on.

"Ma would be terrible angry if I joined up," Todd said. "There isn't anything about army life Ma likes. She wants me to have a different sort of life. She reminded me again this morning that she's got plans for me to go to college someday, like some of her cousins who live in Boston, so I can become a banker or a businessman. She's already teaching me and my sisters Latin verbs and making us read poetry every evening before we go to bed, and—"

A hard lump began to grow in Mike's chest. "You're backing out," he said. "I didn't take you for a quitter."

"I'm not a quitter," Todd insisted. "I was just telling you how Ma would feel if I ran off to join the army."

Through his disappointment Mike shrugged and mumbled, "Then I'll go by myself."

"You're not old enough."

"Neither are you. But age doesn't matter. The Union Army needs musicians to send orders to the troops in battle. We know the drum calls, and you know the bugle. We could help the Union win the war. You know we could."

"Yeah, I guess," Todd said. He glanced at Mike. "How's your mother going to take it?"

"I don't see why Louisa would get mad," Mike answered. "I heard her tell the captain how proud she was of him, before he rode off with his company. But, well, my own ma's different. She won't like my joining the army—I can tell you that right now—and she'll start worrying about me the minute she gets the letter I'm going to write her."

Todd turned to stare at Mike and grinned. "You've got *two* women to worry about whether or not you're getting enough food to eat, or your socks are wet, or there's a Reb on your tail! That's twice as bad as one."

Mike made a face and pretended to groan. "It adds up to more than two," he bragged. "My sisters Frances and Megan will have something to say to me when they find out what I've done, and for all I know, my little sister Peg is old enough to speak her mind on the subject."

Todd chuckled, but Mike grew serious. "Danny now—he's but a year younger than me—Danny would understand. And Petey—he's too little to even think about war."

Once again, Mike was swallowed by a rush of homesickness for his family. He squeezed his eyes shut, seeing their smiling faces, and fought against the pain.

"They're all going to be proud of you," Todd said.

Mike opened his eyes and nodded. He could visualize himself standing tall in the uniform of a Union private, the round-crowned dark blue forage cap cocked so that its black glazed-leather peak sloped down sharply over his eyes. Maybe there'd be a medal on his chest—maybe two or three.

"They're bound to be," he said with a grin. "I'll be the only soldier in the Kelly family."

After a few moments, Todd said, "I guess you're right, Mike. We're bound in duty to help out."

Mike sucked in his breath. "Does that mean you're in?"

"I'm in," Todd said. "When do we go?"

Mike shrugged. "I'm ready to leave now."

Todd shook his head. "No. It would be too easy to send somebody looking for us in the daylight hours. We'll have to leave after dark, probably after they think we're in bed and asleep."

"And have the sentries challenge us?" Mike shook his head. "I've got a better idea. We can leave with the sutlers in late afternoon. Their wagons will be near to empty, and one of them might give us a ride."

Todd pursed his lips as he thought. "A ride would save on shoe leather. It's a good thirty miles or more to Kansas City."

"That's right," Mike said. "And we'll have the drum and your bugle to carry, along with the rest of the things we'll have to take."

Todd looked surprised. "What else do we have to take?"

"Well, a change of clothing, I guess," Mike said, "and a blanket."

"The army issues blankets. Haven't you seen what they've handed out to the new recruits?"

"I guess I haven't paid much attention."

"Well, I have," Todd said. "We'll get a uniform, drawers and socks, shoes, a haversack to carry our rations, a wool-covered tin canteen, and a rubber blanket."

"A *rubber* blanket? What's that for?" Mike asked.

"Keeps everything dry. Sometimes the ground is wet,

and you can spread out the rubber blanket before you make up your bed."

"I've got only about two dollars in coin to call my own," Mike said. "How much have you got?"

Todd looked surprised. "Not much more than that. I guess we'd better take food with us, enough to last until we reach the Second Kansas Infantry and join up."

As he and Todd looked at each other, Mike's heart gave a jump. They were going to enlist. They were really going to do it!

The day passed slowly. That afternoon, companionably chattering to Mike about some of the latest news to reach the fort, Louisa set bread to rise, asking Mike's help in fetching wood for the stove. Mike volunteered to scrub the kitchen floor and sweep the front porch, hoping that if he stayed busy, Louisa wouldn't be able to read his thoughts.

Finally, Louisa said, "It's a very warm day for the end of June, and I'd benefit from a nap." She unbuttoned the high collar of her dress and fanned her neck. "As for you, Mike, I think you're more in need of exercise than study at this moment. We'll delay supper until after sundown, when it's cooler, and go over your lessons this evening. Just be back in time to eat."

Feeling too guilty to meet Louisa's eyes, Mike ducked his head, gave her a quick hug, and ran outside. He'd already set the plan in motion. He'd packed a bundle of clothing, wrapped tightly around letter-writing supplies; he'd lowered the bundle from his window, then tucked it out of sight under the stairway leading to the front porch. As soon as he was sure that Louisa had stretched out on her bed, Mike snatched up his bundle and raced to the barn.

Todd slipped through the door just as Mike was tucking his bundle next to the drum. Todd pointed toward the bale of hay. "I shoved my pack down behind it. I've got food for us, too. Did you get any?"

"I couldn't. Louisa would have been suspicious."

Todd shrugged. "Ma claims I eat all the time. If I *wasn't* into the food, she would have thought something was up."

"I wonder what they'll give us to eat in the army."

"Who cares? We're not joining for home cooking."

Mike laughed, a feverish excitement filling his chest. If all went well, he'd be an officially enlisted musician for the Union Army as soon as tomorrow.

"I wrote Louisa a letter and tucked it under my pillow, where she'll find it tonight," he told Todd.

"I wrote my ma a letter, too," Todd said, "only I gave it to my sister Emily to give to her."

Mike was alarmed. "Won't Emily tell?"

"Nope, because I paid her a dollar. She snuffled and her eyes got red, but then she admitted she was glad I was going. She's still miffed about that frog I put in her bed, among other things." Todd paused, then asked, "What did you say to Louisa?"

"I tried to tell her how grateful I was to her and to the captain for taking me in and how much they mean to me, and then I told her why it's important for me to follow the captain's example and fight for what I believe in. I saw a slave once, captured and in chains, and I'll never forget the awful look in his eyes, like he was already dead. I told Louisa . . ." Mike shook his head and said brusquely, "Well, never mind. I just hope she'll understand."

Todd was matter-of-fact. "Doesn't really matter if she does or not, because you'll be gone."

Mike said nothing, but he knew Todd was wrong. The captain and Louisa were his foster parents, and he loved them almost as much as he loved his own parents.

The tack room was stifling, and the hay made both Mike and Todd sneeze, but they stayed in their hideout. Only when the sun shot long shadows across the parade ground and the sutlers began to cover their unsold merchandise, preparing to leave the fort, did the boys venture out.

Trembling, Mike slung the drum around his neck and picked up the drumsticks with his clothing. "Ready?" he asked Todd.

White-faced, Todd gulped twice before he could answer. "Ready."

The sutlers weren't the only ones to leave the fort. Other tradespeople, salesmen, and visitors found late afternoon a convenient time to depart, and the main gate was crowded with wagons, carriages, and travelers on horseback and on foot. Cautiously, heads down so they wouldn't be recognized, Mike and Todd slid into the crowd.

Mike let out his breath in a whoosh as he realized they were finally out of sight of the guards. Ahead, he spotted a ruddy, smiling sutler who looked familiar.

Running to the side of the wagon, Mike hailed him. "Are you bound for Kansas City?"

"That I am." The sutler tugged on the reins, pulling his horse to a stop at the side of the road. He narrowed his eyes as he studied the boys. "Aren't you needed back at the fort?"

"No," Todd answered quickly, dodging a buggy that passed at a clip. "We're needed by Colonel Mitchell with the Second Kansas Infantry."

The sutler allowed his glance to rest on the drum and bugle. "Things have come to a sad pass when they're signing on mere boys as musicians." But he shrugged as he acknowledged, "Musicians seem to be hard to come by. I've heard some of the companies out of Fort Scott have had to leave without a drummer or bugler."

He gave a jerk of the head toward his nearly empty wagon. "Hop aboard, if you've a mind to, and make yourselves comfortable. It'll be a good ten hours, with time out for resting and watering the horse, afore we reach Kansas City."

Mike and Todd did as they were told, glad for the ride. As the wagon moved out into the rapidly thinning traffic, they settled themselves against the hard wooden sideboards, using their bundles as pillows for their backs.

From his perch high on the front seat of the wagon, the sutler opened a parcel containing a sausage reeking of garlic and a loaf of bread and began to chew noisily. Thankful that he and Todd wouldn't have to offer to share their own supply of food, Mike accepted a chunk of bread and cheese and an apple from his friend and gobbled his supper greedily.

Todd pulled out his pocket watch and peered at it in the dimming light. He breathed on the glass surface, polished it with his sleeve, then tucked it back into his pocket. "Pa gave me this watch," he said, smiling at the recollection.

A strange, gargling noise suddenly came from the front seat. Mike twisted to see if something was the matter and discovered that the sutler had hunched over, his shoulders rounded as a ball.

"He's asleep. He's snoring," Todd whispered as another phlegmy rattle rolled back at them.

"What about the horse? How can he guide him?" Mike whispered.

Todd held his mouth close to Mike's ear. "The horse probably knows the road better than the sutler does. The only thing we'd have to worry about is if the *horse* falls asleep."

Mike buried his face in his arms, trying to smother his bursts of laughter. Finally, when the hysteria of the moment had passed and the sutler snored on undisturbed, Mike stretched out in the wagon bed. Using his bundle of clothes as a pillow, he stared up at the stars, which were shining faintly in the quickly darkening sky.

Todd settled down beside him, but Mike didn't speak. There was too much he wanted to think about. He was on his own, embarked on a great adventure. He had chosen to serve the Union and fight the stubborn-minded southerners who practiced slavery.

Hadn't Da always told him, *Never be afraid to stand up for what you believe is right*? That's what he was doing. With the Union Army so badly in need of musicians, surely they'd accept them. Wouldn't they? Mike groaned involuntarily.

Embarrassed, he quickly turned toward Todd. To Mike's relief, Todd was lying on his side, breathing heavily, sound asleep.

Relax, Mike told himself. *What's done is done. You're on your way, my lad, to join up with the Second Kansas Infantry, and by this time tomorrow night, you'll be a full-fledged, respected member of the Union Army!*

4

Mike and Todd didn't become full-fledged, respected members of the Union Army quite so easily. They parted company with the sutler at close to four in the morning on a dark street in Kansas City. He advised them that Major Samuel Sturgis's battalion still ought to be camped on the outskirts of town.

As the sutler disappeared from view, Mike and Todd stared down the darkened, deserted street and then at each other.

"How are we supposed to reach the outskirts?" Todd asked.

Mike had to smile at Todd's question, which he knew Todd never would have asked if he hadn't been as scared as Mike felt at the moment. "We go in any direction," Mike told him, "except east. East would take us across the river and into Missouri."

"We came from the north," Todd said, beginning to collect himself. "Do you think the sutler drove near to the encampment while we were sleeping?"

Mike blushed at having laughed at the sutler for falling asleep. "It's our best guess," he answered. He turned toward what he hoped was the west. "Let's head west for a ways, then turn north."

They began to walk down the street, their path lit only by the stars. The street narrowed to a lane, and an elderly woman, bent under her shawl as she swept her porch in the first rays of early light, called out, "Where are you boys off to?"

"To find the Second Kansas Infantry," Todd shouted.

The woman shook her fist at them. "Go home and behave yourselves, you abolitionists!"

"Ma'am, this is Kansas—a free state," Mike answered in amazement.

"Free? I'll tell you what freedom is! Until Abraham Lincoln was elected president, this was a free country where every citizen had a right to follow his own beliefs!" she screeched. "Go home! Get along with you!"

Mike and Todd hurried down the lane, turning north when they came to a wagon road. They followed the road for what seemed to be a long while, until it suddenly rose and curved over a hill. Below them, between the hill and the Missouri River, they saw the encampment for which they'd been searching.

Across the plains spread rows and rows of canvas tents, from small pup tents to the large tents used for administration. Already, mounted traffic filled the makeshift roads, some of the riders dressed in the high-crowned, plumed hats, gold-trimmed jackets, and bright blue trousers of the dragoons. Blue-uniformed figures, as small as ants, bustled in all directions. Whorls of dust and plumes of smoke from cooking fires cast a gray haze over a drill unit that already had formed, marching without drumbeat.

Todd drew in a sharp breath, but Mike knew this was no

time to be nervous. "There they are, Todd," he said, "just waiting for us before they march off to battle. It won't take long to get down there and sign our loyalty to the Union."

"There must be close to two thousand of them!" Todd said. "Those Rebs won't stand a chance!"

Mike glanced ahead at a footpath that wound down the hillside. "Come on," he said. "This looks like the quickest way down the hill. Are you ready?"

"Ready!" Todd answered.

The path that left the roadway was steep, but Mike and Todd managed to half-climb, half-slide down the length of it. Finally, they landed on the flat plain, close to the southern boundary of the camp.

Brushing dust from their pants and tugging their jackets into place, they walked briskly toward a cluster of soldiers, where a muscular sergeant stood behind a makeshift desk, checking lists and announcing assignments. He seemed to be the right man to approach.

As he and Todd stepped close, Mike could sense the men eyeing them curiously. He heard an occasional snicker of amusement. Mike nervously clung to the drum hanging in place around his neck and extending to its proper length just above his knees. The drum had brought him here, and the drum was going to assure his acceptance as an army musician.

The sergeant looked up from his papers, his glance sweeping over Mike and Todd before it rested on the drum and bugle. "A musician, are you?" he asked Todd.

"Yes, sir," Todd said. "Bugle and drum."

"How old are you?"

Mike could hear Todd gulp before he answered, "Sixteen, sir."

The sergeant raised one eyebrow, but began at once to rummage through his papers. He pulled out a form, which he handed to Todd. "Colonel Mitchell's got a standing request for musicians. Pay's twelve dollars a month when we've got it. Right now we haven't got it. Sign here for a ninety-day stint, write 'musician' after your name, and report quick as you can to Sergeant Porter to pick up your uniform and supplies. You'll find him at the end of this row of tents."

"Yes, sir!" Todd exclaimed. He scribbled his name before glancing back at Mike. "I'll see you later," he called, then hurried off to find the supply sergeant.

Grinning, the sergeant who had signed up Todd bent down face-to-face with Mike and said, "Sonny boy, you've got to know you're way too young to join the army."

Mike tried to stand as tall as he could and blustered, "I look young for my age, but I'm sixteen."

The sergeant guffawed, as did some of the men standing nearby. "Sixteen, is it? I'm telling you, you're not a day over thirteen."

"I heard you're short of musicians," Mike said. "What does it matter how old I am if I'm needed?"

"What matters is there are rules we gotta go by. Now, run along home, sonny. Your mama is going to be worried about you."

With that, the sergeant turned away from Mike, busying himself with a group of men who had approached his table. Mike didn't budge. *I can't go back*, he told himself in desperation. *The army has to take me. It has to!* He slipped his drumsticks from his pack, straightened his back, and began to beat out the drill calls for advance and retreat.

"Hey, now! What's this?" the sergeant yelled at him, but the flap on a nearby tent opened and a Union officer stepped out. He watched Mike for a minute, then strode to stand next to the sergeant. He held up a hand for silence, and Mike obeyed instantly.

"Captain Dawes, sir," the sergeant said. "I'll send this young rapscallion packing."

"Not so fast," the captain said. He studied Mike. "What's your name, son?"

"Michael Kelly, sir. Everybody calls me Mike."

"Where do you come from, Mr. Kelly?"

Mike's thoughts lurched from the captain and Mrs. Taylor and their home at Fort Leavenworth, to his ma living in St. Joseph, to his first home with Ma and Da and five brothers and sisters in New York. Captain Dawes was waiting for an answer. Mike took a deep breath and said, "I came west out of New York City on one of the orphan trains, sir."

"I've heard of the orphan trains," the captain answered. He studied Mike. "So you're an orphan with no family."

No! Mike hadn't meant to deny his family. While he fumbled for the right words, the captain asked, "How old are you?"

"I—I'm not exactly s-sixteen, Captain Dawes," Mike stuttered.

At this the captain smiled. "Nor even fourteen," he said. "Do you know all the calls?"

"Yes, sir."

"Is that your own drum?"

Mike held it up proudly. "It was given me by a soldier who brought it through the Indian wars."

"Sir, the age rule—" the sergeant began.

But Captain Dawes interrupted. "The age rule applies to regular soldiers, Sergeant Gridley. A musician isn't a regular soldier and doesn't carry a gun. My unit is in sore need of a musician, so sign Mr. Kelly up. Have him report to me in uniform on the parade ground in half an hour."

Mike could hardly keep from jumping and shouting with joy. "Thank you, Captain Dawes!" he managed to stammer.

As he bent to sign the paper that Sergeant Gridley shoved under his nose, he felt a great goodwill toward everyone—even Sergeant Gridley. But before Mike could open his mouth to say so, Gridley barked, "You can inquire as to what the supply sergeant might have for you, Mikey boy. I'm afraid it won't be much. Far as I know, he didn't order any uniforms in children's sizes."

"From what you're wearing, I'd guess he has a good stock of wide-bottomed pants," Mike shot back.

As some of the soldiers in earshot guffawed, Mike hurried away, following the route Todd had taken. He'd come to fight Rebs, not loudmouthed sergeants, he reminded himself, and it certainly didn't make much sense to take on a man three times his size.

Within a few minutes he found the supply sergeant, who groaned when he saw the size of the newly appointed musician.

"You'll need your sturdy belt to hold up the smallest size pants we've got," he said, "and I can't do much about a jacket without rolling up the sleeves."

"I'm growing fast," Mike said.

"It's not fast enough," the supply sergeant said. He went through his stock, finally coming up with oversize drawers and socks, a jacket and pants, a forage cap with a musician's brass bugle on the front, a canteen, a woolen blanket, and a rubber blanket. "I can't help you with boots," he told Mike. "We didn't get any boots, and how some of these men are going to march for miles in shoes that are falling apart . . . well, never mind. Report back to Sergeant Gridley for your assignment. Although he hasn't got enough tents. You'll find yourself sharing one with at least three other men, maybe four. When one man rolls over, everyone rolls over."

Mike laughed, but the supply sergeant shook his head sadly.

What does it matter? Mike thought. *The weather's warm. I can make my bed outside, under the stars.* Slapping his cap on his head, making sure the brim dipped over his forehead at a jaunty angle, Mike carried his supplies back to Sergeant Gridley, who grinned as he gave Mike his tent assignment. Thankful that the sergeant was a man who could take a joke, Mike easily found the tent and changed into his uniform.

Just as the supply sergeant had warned, Mike had to roll

up the sleeves and pants legs. He felt as if he were dressed in Captain Taylor's clothes. *I may not fill your shoes yet, but someday I'll make you proud of me,* he thought, smiling to himself.

Out on the parade ground Captain Dawes took one look at Mike and said, "Can you use a needle and thread?"

"No, sir," Mike said. He tried to ignore the grins and joking comments of the men assembled for drill, but his face burned with embarrassment.

"Then we'll find someone who can," Dawes told him. "We'll do our best to outfit you the way a soldier should be outfitted. Now, let's get these men in shape. Sound the call to drill, Mr. Kelly."

"Yes, sir," Mike said, grateful to this fine man. He was determined to do Captain Dawes's bidding forever. He'd stand by his side, drumming the calls in the thick of battle. Mike flourished his drumsticks and beat out the sharp roll that signaled the men to fall into line and stand at attention.

For half an hour they worked until the men learned to interpret the drumbeats that carried their officer's instructions from *advance* to *retreat.* "That was good work, Mr. Kelly," the captain said at the end of the drill, loudly enough for his troop to hear.

"Thank you, sir," Mike answered. He reddened again, but this time with pleasure.

Then Captain Dawes announced, "Tonight will be a good time to write letters to those you've left at home. Tomorrow, under Major Sturgis's command of the Fourth Battalion, our Second Kansas Infantry will begin a trek into southern Missouri to join forces with General Lyon's brigade."

Mike vaguely heard Captain Dawes say that the march would involve more than two thousand men just in the Fourth Brigade alone, but Mike's mind was on the letters he needed to write. He'd left one for Louisa, but by all rights he needed to tell Ma what he'd done, and he couldn't leave out Frances and Petey, Megan, Peg, and Danny. He needed to know they'd be thinking of him and praying for him. Good thinking to have tucked writing supplies into his pack! No matter what, Mike promised himself, he would write those letters before lights out.

But soon Mike saw that finding time to write letters would be more difficult than he imagined. Nor did he have time to search for Todd and share his great news that he was now a member of the Union Army, too. Immediately after supper, Sergeant Gridley cornered him.

"You don't think your work is over, do you, boy? Any soldier bold enough to talk back to his superior certainly must have energy to carry water for the horses and firewood for the cook. And when you're done with that, there's more to do." *So the sergeant wasn't open to a bit of fun,* Mike thought. He'd have to be more careful to keep his mouth shut about wide-bottomed pants and such in the future.

Not until after drumming *tattoo,* the evening roll call designed to discourage deserters, could Mike escape his chores for the night and head for his tent. To his surprise and delight, Todd was there, spreading his rubber blanket on the ground.

A burly corporal with a dark beard as thick as a bush laughed and said to Mike, "Sergeant Gridley thought you boys would like to be together." He held out a hand as big as a beefsteak first to Mike, then to Todd. "The name is Harley Botts."

Two other men squeezed into the tent, and Corporal Botts introduced the other tent mates: a lanky, straw-haired eighteen-year-old named Ben Doland, and a shorter, plump, balding man named Billy Whitley.

Then, to Mike's surprise, Harley pulled a needle, thread, and scissors out of his jacket pocket. "I volunteered to do something to make that uniform fit you a mite better, Mike. Take off the jacket, and I'll see what I can do."

"You can sew?" Mike asked. He had seen women taking dainty stitches as they darned and mended, but the idea of this huge man doing the same was astounding.

"It's a skill that's come in handy more often than not," Harley said, and he proceeded to fold, bend, and cut, then stitch with a needle that almost disappeared between his large thumb and finger. Mike watched, fascinated.

By the time Mike's pants were taken in at the waist and shortened at the legs, Todd had filled him in on what he'd done during the day.

"Not half a sight as much as I had to do," Mike grumbled, and explained his run-in with Sergeant Gridley.

Todd whooped with laughter, but Harley reminded the boys that a well-run army called for firm military order among the troops. "Sergeant Will Gridley's a fair man," Harley said, a twinkle in his eyes softening the seriousness of his words, "but it's best that you keep a civil tongue in your head, Michael."

"I will," he assured Harley. But Mike's repentance was short-lived as Ben and Billy joined in the conversation about what life in the army was like for volunteers.

"There'll be bugs in the bedding, and how they bite!"

"Don't be expecting home cooking. You could just as easy chew through a harness as through some of the meat we get."

They added a bit of good-natured gossip about one officer or another, and even Harley couldn't help but smile. The companionship made Mike feel a real part of the Union Army, bedbugs and all. Hearing Todd chuckle, Mike was sure that Todd felt the same way.

Harley informed the boys that Todd would be directly under Colonel Mitchell's command, and Mike under the same command but with Captain Dawes's troop. Together, as part of the Second Kansas Infantry, they'd leave in the morning in a march to fight the Rebs.

"Tomorrow," Todd said.

"Tomorrow," Mike echoed, his heartbeat quickening. He reached into his pack for his writing supplies. With a war to be won, who knew when next he'd find time to write?

5

No one needed to wake Mike the next morning. He was up, dressed, and in position before the duty officer arrived. Along with the other drummers throughout the camp, he beat out the rrrrat-a-tat of *reveille* to call the sleeping men to assembly.

The soldiers ate breakfast quickly, dismantled the tents, and stored them in the long train of wagons, which also carried ammunition, field equipment, and other supplies.

The air crackled with excitement, and Mike's breathing quickened as uniformed men, full packs on their backs, assembled at the sound of the drum roll.

Dragoons, resplendent in their colorful uniforms, and blue-uniformed riders in Company One of the Second Kansas Mounted formed their units on the road, eager for orders to begin the march. Even the horses caught the excitement, snorting and tossing their heads as artillery was wheeled into place. Over the creak of wagon wheels, the shouted commands, and the overall noisy bustle, five companies of cavalry, six companies of regular infantry and dragoons, and ten companies of Kansas volunteers received their orders and fell into line to begin the trek toward Grand River in southwestern Missouri.

Dust from the horses and wagons rose like a cloud. Soon a fine gray powder covered the eyebrows and beards of Mike's fellow marchers. The drums set the pace for the first few minutes, after which the men fell into a slower, less measured walk. Some of the soldiers were fit and walked without complaint, but a few stragglers groaned and lagged behind.

"Was there ever heat like this?" Billy complained. He pulled off his forage cap to wipe his bald head with a muddy cotton handkerchief. Rivulets of sweat mixed with the dust on his face and trickled down in dirty streams.

Harley Botts spoke up. "Better get used to it. You've got a long walk ahead of you."

"I was countin' on fightin' the enemy, not doin' all this walkin'," Billy grumbled.

"All well and good," Harley countered, "but you've got to get to the Rebs first, and the only way to do that is to put one foot ahead of the other and keep goin'."

A messenger on horseback raced past, kicking up new clouds of dust that made Mike cough and rub his eyes. His stomach growled loudly, and he realized how hungry he was.

Harley turned to Mike. "They should have plenty of provisions for our noon meal, but when supplies run low they'll set us to foragin'."

"Foraging? What does that mean?" Mike asked.

"It means stoppin' at farmhouses and requisitioning whatever foodstuffs they've put by, whether it's corn from their fields, potatoes in their cellars, or hens from their barnyards."

"Do we buy them?" Mike thought of the pitifully small amount of money he carried with him.

Harley grinned. "No. We help ourselves. The citizens should be glad enough to aid the soldiers who're goin' off to battle to protect them."

"But to take a farmer's chickens is stealing," Mike protested. The memory of his copper theft in New York City and all the trouble it had caused filled him with pain.

"Which is easier—to give a few chickens, or to give a son to battle?" Harley asked.

Mike thought about his Kansas bunkmates who had left their farms and volunteered to fight. "Some families give both."

"All the more reason, then, to feed Union soldiers."

"I guess so," Mike answered, but he was glad for a loud interruption to this conversation.

"Halt!" a sergeant called. Stomachs growling, the men lined up for their rations of dried beef and hardtack.

Hearing the lapping of a small creek, Mike ran to it as soon as he had eaten. He let the bubbling water run over his hands as he refilled his water bottle. Then he pulled off his cap and splashed the cool water over his sweaty face and neck until they were clean. His pack and drum seemed to have gotten ten times heavier over the course of the march. He would have given anything for a chance to crawl into a spot of shade under the bank along the creek bed for a long, deep sleep, but he barely had time to imagine such relief when he heard the sharp call, "Formation!" and the march began again.

Mike trudged along, hour after hour, stopping only to wait as messengers on horseback raced at breakneck speed from the front of the line to the back and then to the front again. Conversations among those around him began to lag. Nothing seemed important enough or interesting enough to talk about, especially through that constant, powdery, choking dust.

Finally, to Mike's great relief, the long straggling line of marchers was instructed to make camp for the night.

Mike still had to drum the calls to supper, then *tattoo* and *taps.* As soon as Mike had finished, Todd joined him, and the two of them found a patch of relatively smooth ground where they could spread out their rubber blankets. They beat the dust from their clothes, took off their shoes, and stretched out, rolling their woolen blankets up and over them.

Todd yawned noisily and squirmed on his mat. "I'll tell you this much," he said. "This is nothing like the feather mattress on my bed at home."

"Home . . ." Mike repeated. But before he could finish the thought, he fell into a sound sleep.

He awoke early in the morning, as light first streaked the sky. He scrambled to get dressed and took his place with his drum. The moment he heard the command, Mike woke the sleeping men in his company with the sharp beat of his drum.

The march, with so many men and so much equipment to move, proceeded slowly. Mike could only guess at the reasons for the countless stops.

The heat became almost unbearable, but even an occasional rain shower, welcome as it was, was a mixed blessing. Musty wet woolen clothing, steaming dry in the sunlight, only worsened the stench of men who couldn't remember when they'd last laid eyes on a bathtub. Mike crinkled his nose, eager for this exhausting, boring march to be over and the battle to begin.

During the rest periods, the soldiers spoke of their loved ones, and some mournfully sang songs that reminded them of home. Mike, too, had pangs of longing for his family, but he worried most about Todd, who wore an expression of unrelieved sadness. As Billy reminisced about his wife and two small boys, a strangled sound, suspiciously like a sob, escaped from Todd.

"I've got five sisters," Todd mumbled. "They're sweet

little girls, all of them depending on me for protection ever since our father's company was sent off to Virginia."

Harley was blunt. "Then why didn't you stay home with them? Why'd you sign up?"

As Todd hesitated, Mike quickly spoke. "It won't do his sisters any good if those Confederate Rebels win the war. What might happen to our country then?" He clapped a firm hand on Todd's shoulder.

Todd lifted his chin. "That's right," he said. "Mike and me—we heard the Federals were short of musicians. We knew the calls, so we were bound to serve."

"It would be nothing short of pure selfishness to hide our talents," Mike added.

Ben hooted at the bragging, but Mike insisted, "Out on the battlefield, you'll be mighty glad our bugle and drum are there to lead you on."

Mike's exhaustion vanished. He grinned proudly at Todd, and Todd smiled back. But that night, after most of the men had gone to sleep and Mike lay awake imagining himself drumming bravely as he spurred the men in Captain Dawes's company to attack, he heard muffled sobbing from under Todd's blanket.

Mike reached out a hand, wanting to comfort his friend, but he pulled back. He gave a couple of soft pretend snores, hoping Todd would think he was asleep, and lay very still. In just a few minutes Todd's sobs ended, gradually turning into a slow, measured breathing as he slept.

Mike could well remember what it was like to shed secret tears. When he was adopted as a foster child by the stern, unkind Mr. Friedrich, he'd spent many sleepless nights crying for Ma and the rest of his family, grieving over the circumstances that had caused them to be separated. Megan had been taken by a couple who farmed on the Kansas prairie. His oldest sister, Frances Mary, and five-year-old Petey went with a childless couple from northeastern Kansas, and Danny and Peg had been chosen by a farmer and his wife who lived not too far from St. Joseph.

It had been Danny who'd worked out a way for Ma to come west and join them, but only Peg lived with Ma and her new husband, John Murphy. A hearty Irishman, John might have been a loving father, but he couldn't financially support all Ma's children, so Mike scarcely knew him.

But after the heartache of losing Da and living with Mr. Friedrich, Mike had once again found a father. Along had come Captain Joshua Taylor—strong, brave Captain Taylor —who with his wife Louisa had taken Mike to raise as a son.

Mike sighed. Just when he had needed a father the most, Captain Taylor had gone off to defend the Union. If the war could be shortened by a quick defeat of the South, then maybe life would become peaceful and Mike would again know the joys and comforts of having a father. But until then . . .

Mike drifted off to sleep, and in his dreams a man—at times Captain Taylor and at times Da—draped a comforting arm around Mike's shoulders.

The brigade had been marching for a week under a July sun that burned hotter than a campfire, when orders were given to forage for the evening meal. With a foraging detachment led by Sergeant Gridley, Mike was instructed to head for a nearby group of farmhouses.

"What will we do—request whatever they can spare?" Mike asked Sergeant Gridley.

The sergeant's lip curled with amusement. "*I'm* the one who'll do the talking—not you, Mikey boy."

One of the other soldiers, not too many years older than Mike, snickered. "We don't request. We *take.*"

Mike looked the soldier in the eye. "You mean we *steal.*"

"Simmer down," the sergeant ordered Mike. "These are wartime conditions. We follow emergency rules."

"I lived on a farm for a while," Mike said. "A farmer can't survive if we take away what he grows and sells."

Sergeant Gridley stopped and faced Mike. "How about helping our *soldiers* to survive? You've seen the great number in our brigade. How do you propose feeding them on a long march? Even with the sutlers' wagons and the local merchants coming to sell foodstuffs, we can't provide enough to fill the bellies of thousands of hungry men."

Mike felt his face redden, and he mumbled agreement. He couldn't imagine how much food it would take to feed an army, and it was true—the men had to have three meals a day to keep up their strength for the march.

Sergeant Gridley motioned Mike to walk by his side, as he and the eight other soldiers with him climbed the slope leading to a trim white house with a large barn behind it. "During wartime, Mike, people can lose everything—their houses, their possessions, and even their families—but they manage to survive and rebuild their lives. Taking a small amount of food is little to ask of a patriotic farmer. You'll see."

As they approached the house, a woman stepped out onto the porch. "We're Federal!" she called out. "We mean you no harm!"

"Ma'am," the sergeant said, doffing his cap as he stood below the porch steps, his men behind him, "we're in need of food."

"As are we," she said bitterly.

"Will you call your husband, please, so I might speak with him?"

The woman leaned against the porch railing, and her stiff-backed courage seemed to slip away as she sighed. "My husband's somewhere in eastern Missouri with General Lyon's forces," she said.

"That's commendable, ma'am," Sergeant Gridley told her. "Is there another man around your property we might speak to?"

"My son's gone from home, too," she answered softly—

almost as though she were talking to herself, Mike thought. "Ab was bound and determined to run off to join the Missouri State Guard under Sterling Price."

"A Rebel sympathizer?" Mike blurted out, then clapped a hand over his mouth.

"Ma'am," Sergeant Gridley said, "we'll respect the privacy of your house, but if you've got preserves put by, we'd appreciate it if you'd bring them out. In the meantime we're in need of potatoes or other vegetables from your root cellar. And if you've got chickens . . ."

The woman closed her eyes and waved a hand toward the barn. "Go ahead," she said. "Take what you need. Just remember that my two daughters and I will need something to live on until our cash crop of oats can be harvested."

"Thank you, ma'am," the sergeant said. He quickly turned to the men in his detachment and ordered groups to go in various directions. Finally he came to Mike. "There's bound to be chickens and eggs," he said. "You may find them in a henhouse, maybe in the barn. Take a look. Collect whatever you can."

Reluctantly, Mike trudged to the rear of the house. He saw no signs of a henhouse, but he heard a clucking coming from inside the closed doors of the barn, so he swung one of the big doors open and entered.

The dimness inside the barn was such a contrast to the bright sunlight that for a moment Mike couldn't see, and he squinted. But something brown and squawking practically ran over his feet and into an empty horse stall.

A fat hen! And where there was one there were bound to be others, along with the eggs they'd laid so far today. Mike, his eyes growing accustomed to the sparse light, followed the hen into the stall. When he bent down and made a grab for her, the hen loudly complained and tried to flap her wings in protest.

As he rose, he heard a young girl's voice tearfully protesting, "Janie! He's got Miz Toozie!"

Mike looked up to see the child clutching the skirt of an older girl. Then he saw the gun. The older girl gazed at Mike from behind the long barrel of a rifle aimed right at his face.

6

"PUT DOWN Miz Toozie," the older girl said, "and don't you dare reach for your gun."

"I haven't got a gun," Mike answered.

"You expect me to believe that? You're a soldier, aren't you?"

"I'm a drummer."

She opened the eye she'd been squinting as she aimed and studied Mike. "You're only a boy," she said with surprise.

"I'm old enough to have signed up with the Union Army!"

"I don't care how old you are," the girl said calmly, as she leveled the rifle again. "If you don't let go of Miz Toozie, I'm going to shoot you."

The girl was as tall as Mike, and he guessed she was probably only a couple of years older than he. Her brown hair was caught back into a braid, but her flower-patterned dress had faded to the palest of blues, with patches sewn over spots where the fabric had worn through.

The thought that this family clearly couldn't afford to lose their chickens flashed through Mike's mind. But as he stared at the rifle, he instinctively gripped the hen more tightly. "Listen to me, Janie," he said. "Your mother gave us permission to take some of your supplies to feed our brigade."

"Miz Toozie is not a supply! She's my friend!" the little girl wailed, and burst into tears.

"Hush, Lettie," Janie murmured. But she kept the rifle steady as she said to Mike, "We've barely got enough put by to get us through the winter."

"We've barely got enough to get us through the day," he countered.

"That's not our fault."

"It's not ours, either. There's a long march ahead of us, and we have to be fed."

"But not with Miz Toozie."

As Mike's initial fear began to subside, his curiosity took over. She might threaten him with the rifle, but surely she wouldn't kill him, would she? "Your ma said that your father is fighting with the Union and your brother's with the Rebs. You wouldn't want either of them to go hungry."

For just an instant Janie's face twisted in pain. "That has nothing to do with you."

"Their companies have to forage for food the same way mine does." He began to parrot what he'd been told. "It takes a lot of food to feed an army. Men without food would be too weak to fight, and—"

"Stop it!" Janie shouted. She angrily slammed the butt of the rifle against the hard-packed floor of the barn. Mike ducked and winced, waiting for the blast.

But nothing happened, and Janie mumbled, "It wasn't loaded."

"You gave me a scare," Mike said, and he couldn't help grinning, mostly from the relief of not being shot.

"*Please* don't take Miz Toozie," Lettie begged. "She's been my pet forever and ever, and Ma promised she'd never be eaten."

Mike sighed. Lettie was so sweet and trusting, she reminded him of Peg, when she was little. "Have you got other hens?" he asked.

"Fluff-fluff and Pansy and Redtop and—"

Mike cringed. "Don't tell me their names!" He hated the idea of eating an animal with a pet name.

Lettie's eyes widened hopefully and she chattered, "And Brownie, and our pigs are named Mr. Grump and—"

Janie put a hand over her sister's mouth. "Take what you have to," she said to Mike, "but please don't take Lettie's pet."

Mike handed the still-struggling hen to the little girl, who whispered a few soothing words to Miz Toozie.

"Thank you," Janie said, and turned to leave the barn.

Mike called after her, "Can you help me collect the other hens and show me where they nest?"

The corners of Janie's mouth twisted. "Help you? Not for anything in the world! You're going to have to perform your highway robbery by yourself!"

Mike knew how much his company needed the hens, but he took Janie's words to heart. "There may be others who'll come into your barn to look around," he told Lettie. "You'd better hide yourself and your hen someplace where they can't find you."

"Out in the oatfield," Lettie whispered.

"Don't tell *me*, either," Mike cautioned.

Without a word, Lettie slipped out a narrow door in back of the barn, and Mike set about his task.

The detachments returned with a haul of potatoes, squash, turnips, chickens, and eggs, as well as jars of preserved carrots, snap beans, and apple butter. Storing most of the food for future meals, the men prepared the perishable foods for a feast. They roasted plucked chickens on spits over the fires, buried potatoes in the ashes for slow baking, and tossed whole pale turnips and green pattipan squash into pots of boiling water.

When the meal was ready, the soldiers ate hungrily, but Mike chewed his chicken with great difficulty. What if they were eating Brownie or Pansy or Redtop? He almost choked at the thought.

Later, at *tattoo*, two of the volunteers in Captain Dawes's company—Amos Dailey and Ezra McNabb—failed to answer the roll call.

"Does anyone know the whereabouts of either or both of these men?" Sergeant Gridley asked.

Ben Doland stepped forward. "They set off for home. They didn't know this march was gonna take such an infernal long time, and they got to get ready for harvestin'."

"Listen to me, men," Captain Dawes announced. "Those of you who are volunteers must remember that you're not free to leave whenever you wish. Each of you signed on to serve for ninety days. That's a contract you made with President Abraham Lincoln, the government of the United States, and the Union Army. Do you all understand?"

No one said a word, but after the men had been dismissed, Mike heard Ben mutter, "Crops don't wait for no man, includin' the president himself. Can't say I blame Amos and Ezra one bit."

"Don't *you* take it into your head to run off," Harley told Ben. "That would make you a deserter, too."

"Deserter? That's a hard word to use for a man whose wife took sick, like Amos's did."

"He had a contract with the army," Harley insisted. "We need every man we can get if we're going to beat those Confederates."

"Yeah? When's that gonna be?" Ben asked. "We ain't

seen any fightin' so far. We just walk and walk, and my shoes are gonna fall apart soon."

A few days later, Major Sturgis's battalion joined General Lyon's forces at Grand River, as the two Union forces had planned. Mike was eager to catch a glimpse of General Lyon. Harley, who'd known Nathaniel Lyon when they were both stationed at Fort Riley, Kansas, had described Lyon to Mike: "The general's known to be narrow-minded, with a temper that goes off like a rocket when things don't go the way he thinks they should."

"I take it you don't like him," Mike had said.

"I didn't say that," Harley countered. "The man's honest in all his dealings, and always truthful." He paused, then added, "Still, his discipline is often more strict than need be, and he's a hard taskmaster."

"Well? What is it?" Mike asked. "Do you like him or don't you?"

Harley's broad shoulders heaved in a mighty shrug. "General Lyon is our commanding officer. Even though it's hard to find a man who likes him, it's not for me to speak my mind about him."

Mike looked away so Harley couldn't catch his grin. The turns Harley went through to avoid saying he disliked the man!

But when Mike finally encountered the general, he didn't grin. Though the general wasn't exceptionally tall, his features were forbidding: deep-set eyes, a long narrow nose, and dark thick hair and beard.

It wasn't only the general's appearance that was intimidating. As he strode back and forth in front of the temporary headquarters and expounded in an angry voice that hurt Mike's ears, Mike was glad he wouldn't have any direct dealings with the man.

"I have requested over and over that I be sent more troops. At least half my strength of over seven thousand men are three-month volunteers whose time will soon be up."

That wasn't news to Mike. He'd heard much the same from Harley, but he perked up when General Lyon said, "My spies inform me that Confederate generals Ben McCulloch and N. Bart Pearce are planning to bring their Arkansas troops to join General Sterling Price and his Missouri State Guard. That will mean the massing of at least eleven thousand Confederate officers and soldiers just below Springfield. If they attack us and we are unable to repel them, we will lose Missouri."

Mike choked down the lump that rose in his throat. Lose Missouri? That couldn't be!

Without waiting for a reply from his officers, Lyon continued, his voice becoming even more tense: "Our men have not been paid, and the condition of their uniforms is deplorable! They are badly off for clothing, and the want of shoes makes them unfit for marching."

Mike well remembered the uniforms of cheap wool shoddy that a crooked clothing supplier had sent to Fort Leavenworth. What had gone wrong that the Union Army had not enough men and not enough proper supplies?

Soon word spread among the soldiers that Union General Sigel's regiment had been beaten in a skirmish at Carthage. Mike wasn't the only soldier who was disheartened by the news of a Confederate win and felt eager to even the score by supporting General Sigel's troops. But Sigel had retreated to Springfield, and General Lyon decided to join him there. Major Sturgis's battalion set up camp at Pond Springs, a few miles west of Springfield, to wait for further orders.

Ben sighed loudly. "More walkin'."

"Take it like a man," Harley told him. "You don't hear the boys complainin', do you?" He winked at Mike, and Mike smiled at the praise.

Then after all their struggles and uncertainty, good news came at last. Arriving in Pond Springs on July 13, the battalion learned of a Union victory on July 11 at the Battle of Rich Mountain in western Virginia.

While cheers went up, Mike nearly burst with pride. Captain Taylor was in Virginia! He and his company had probably fought at Rich Mountain. And they had won!

Soon, Mike was sure, he, too, would be involved in a Union victory. Those Confederates, swarming in great numbers up from Arkansas into southern Missouri, would turn tail and go running back!

Although there were plenty of duties to keep Mike busy, he noticed that he wasn't the only one who was restless. Why should they have such a long wait? The Confederates were within a day's march, ready to strike.

"If I were General Lyon, I wouldn't wait for those Rebs to take action. I'd strike first," Mike told Todd as they sat by a campfire one evening, both of them with paper and envelopes on their lap, ready to write again to their families.

"The general has spies and scouts. He knows what's going on, which is more than you do," Todd snapped. Todd had never spoken that way to Mike, and his words cut like a bayonet.

For an instant Todd looked stricken, too. "Sorry, Mike," he murmured. "It's hard to think about going into battle. Just between you and me, sometimes I wish we hadn't joined up."

"Would you have wanted to sit out the war, safely back at the fort with your little sisters?"

"N-no," Todd said slowly.

"There, you see?" Mike countered. "Our Union forces will soon lick the Rebs, the war will be over, and we'll return home with a row of medals across our chests."

Todd had to smile. "All right, Mike. If you say so." He licked the end of his pencil and began to write.

Mike leaned over Todd's shoulder. "That's the second letter to your ma this week."

Todd grinned. "There's not much else to do but write letters or play cards, is there? And Ma'd have a fit if I so much as picked up a deck of cards."

Mike set to his own letter-writing, bragging to Danny about the upcoming battle and the way they were going to defeat those Rebs.

On Saturday evening, July 20, the one-armed, tough, and courageous Union General Sweeny commanded twelve hundred men who had been assembled in a mix of infantry, cavalry, and artillery to break up a camp of secessionists at the small southern Missouri town of Forsyth. Mike was among the assembled men; Todd was among those who stayed behind.

Among the soldiers, Mike sloshed along roads that rain had turned into beds of mud. His forage cap, protected by an oilskin cover, remained dry, but the rest of his clothes were soaked by the rain. *This is it*, he thought. *This is what I've been waiting for.* Close to Captain Dawes's side, ready to send any order through his drum calls, Mike envisioned himself helping to guide the men through the fight.

It took two days to cover the forty-five miles of hilly, rugged countryside between Springfield and Forsyth, and the rain changed to a hot dry sun that seemed to beckon every biting, flying bug in the county. The stink of drying wool and sweating bodies overpowered the cleaner fragrances of wet earth and washed meadow grasses.

Riders on horseback brought the command to a halt. Word swept down the line faster than a grass fire. A handful of Rebs had challenged General Sweeny's mounted advance guard, but the guard had captured two of them instead.

General Sweeny directed Captain Stanley of the cavalry to take his two companies and the mounted Kansans and surround the town. The artillery and infantry were to follow.

To Mike's disappointment, the battle was over before the Second Kansas Infantry arrived, and on July 24 he found himself back in Springfield. "Wasn't much to it," he complained to Todd. "There were only a hundred and fifty state guards, headquartered in the courthouse. They fired on the mounted troopers as they rode into town, but when the troopers fired back, the Rebs fled into the hills, hiding in the trees and underbrush. The artillery flushed them out of those woods like a covey of quail."

Todd looked hopeful. "Maybe the rest of the Rebs will run off, too."

"Sure," Mike said, puffing out his chest and looking wise. "All we have to do is throw a scare into them."

"I wish it had been like that at Bull Run," Todd said, and Mike saw the worry in Todd's eyes and a drawn, frightened look on his face.

"What's Bull Run?" Mike asked, wishing he hadn't been so full of his own story that he hadn't seen that something terrible was bothering his friend. "What are you talking about?"

"You didn't hear the news?" Todd answered. "Our Union forces took a terrible beating from the Confederates at what they're calling the Battle of Bull Run, near Manassas, Virginia. A woman spy for the Confederacy told them the Union Army's plans. We should have won, but instead there were many . . . many Union soldiers killed."

Mike tried to swallow. His mouth was dry, and his throat tightened with fear. "Captain Taylor and your pa, Todd . . . they would have been there, wouldn't they? Do you know if they . . . ?" Mike couldn't continue.

Todd's eyes filmed with pain as he shook his head.

Mike clenched and unclenched his clammy hands. "I *have* to know. I'll ask Captain Dawes how we can find out."

"You aren't going to tell him about Captain Taylor adopting you, are you?"

"No," Mike said. "There has to be another way." As he headed toward his company headquarters, he murmured, "Don't worry. By the time I find Captain Dawes, I'll come up with an idea."

7

HIS HEART POUNDING, Mike found the captain leaving the headquarters tent. The muscles in his face were tight, and dark circles shadowed his eyes.

Quickly stepping to the captain's side, Mike blurted out, "Sir, I have a friend in camp named Todd Blakely. His father's Captain John Blakely, serving with Captain Joshua Taylor in Virginia."

Captain Dawes's eyes lit with recognition. "Josh Taylor was a classmate of mine at West Point."

Mike was cold, even though sweat tickled his neck and backbone. "What I mean, sir . . . Todd is awful worried about Captain Tay—that is, his father *and* Captain Taylor. Is there any chance of knowing whether they were at Bull Run, and whether they . . . uh . . ." Mike couldn't finish.

Captain Dawes clapped a hand on Mike's shoulder. "I can tell you about Captain Taylor, because we were just reading correspondence about the battle and its unfortunate outcome. Josh's name stood out to me because he's a friend. He survived the battle with honor. As a matter of fact, he received a field promotion to major."

A rush of relief and thankfulness left Mike light-headed. His voice cracked as he asked, "And Todd's father? Captain Blakely? Do you know what happened to him?"

Captain Dawes hesitated. "I wish I had good news for your friend, but as yet I haven't. We weren't sent a list of casualties."

Mike slowly made his way back to where Todd was waiting. "They don't have a list of casualties yet," Mike said. "But that doesn't mean anything bad happened to . . . to either your father or mine. We've got to keep thinking that they both survived the battle with honor."

Tears flooded Todd's eyes, and he rubbed them away angrily as he dropped cross-legged to the ground. After a few moments he said, "Mike, we'll be going into battle soon, and I've been thinking—not everybody lives through a battle to tell about it."

"Don't say that!" Mike scolded as he squatted next to Todd. "It's not right."

"It's right to face the truth," Todd said.

Mike shook his head. "It's just asking for trouble," he insisted.

Todd put a hand on Mike's arm. "I don't own much of any value, but . . ." He reached into his pocket and pulled out his simple gold-plated pocket watch, which had been dented by baby teeth. "You know that my pa gave this to me on my last birthday." Todd bit his lip hard enough to leave marks before he asked, "Mike, if I'm killed in battle, will you take my watch, and when you once again reach home, will you give it to my sister Emily?"

"Todd! You're not going to get killed!"

Todd tightened his grip on Mike's arm, and Mike winced.

"You've got to promise, Mike! Promise!"

"All right," Mike said. "I promise. I'll do whatever you want."

Solemnly, Mike and Todd shook hands.

"And now," Mike said, trying hard to sound cheerful and hearty, "let's decide how we'll celebrate once the battle's over and the victory's been won."

"Celebrate with what?" Todd asked.

Mike winked. "Maybe with a nice roasted turkey. I saw a few in a field a ways back. Now, wouldn't turkey taste good along with applesauce? I think I'd dive in headfirst. Gobble, gobble, gobble."

Todd couldn't help smiling, and Mike was cheered.

When the mail arrived, both Mike and Todd received their first letters from their families, and Todd's good humor seemed completely restored.

Like many of the soldiers who had received mail, Mike found a place apart from his friends and settled down to read the letters over and over in private.

Mike read Louisa Taylor's letter first. In no uncertain terms she wrote that she was frantic about Mike, who was much too young to serve his country. Yet she added, "There is nothing that can be done about it now, so I can only say that my prayers and love will follow you wherever you go."

In the next letter, Ma gave Mike a good blunt scolding before her words lost their edge and became as tender as Mike remembered. "My impulsive, my adventuresome son," Ma wrote, "I guess I should have expected to see you leap to be one of the first to serve your country. Just remember, you are still a boy, not yet a man. Stay away from those who drink and gamble with cards, choose your companions wisely, and don't forget to pray. Throughout each and every day, I'll be praying for you." Ma sent her everlasting love and included a funny note from Peg, who wrote a gleeful description of mean Mr. Crandon tripping and falling facedown into a mud puddle. Mike would never forget Mr. Crandon—the stuffy bank president who had wanted to send him back to New York—and prison. He hoped he never met up with that man again.

There was a short letter from Megan, who promised to write every week, and a longer letter from Frances, who didn't scold, as Mike thought she might. She longed for the slave issue to be settled once and for all, the war to be over soon, and Mike to return safely to his home with the Taylors.

There was no letter yet from Danny, but Mike wasn't worried about his brother, who'd have to take a long drive to town in order to post his letter.

Soon Todd, with a wide smile on his face, joined Mike and dropped to the ground next to him. "Ma got it all off her chest, and then she began writing loving things and telling me how she was arranging with her brother Peter to have me live with his family in Boston when the war is over." Todd chuckled. "All I care about is that Ma's got over being mad at me. From now on everything's gonna be all right."

Todd punched Mike's arm, Mike punched back, and they scuffled, rolled, yelled, and laughed until two men plucked them apart, dangling them in the air by their belts.

"Cut out the fighting! You want to get in trouble?"

Harley's deep voice broke in: "Leave the boys alone. Don't you remember when you were their age and havin' fun?"

And so the men dumped Mike and Todd on the ground, where—still laughing—they scrambled to pick up their mail.

During the next few days camp life followed its usual pattern, with one exception. General Lyon, concerned about protecting the citizens of Springfield from unwarranted raids, issued an order temporarily forbidding foraging. As a result, all soldiers under his command were existing on half-rations. The soldiers' empty bellies made the long wait to fight the Confederates seem all the longer.

"General Frémont took charge of the western army," Harley said during one of the men's countless card games, "and I heard tell that he won't send Lyon the troops he's been begging for. Lyon is afraid of getting beat without the extra men, and he's hoping Frémont will change his mind."

Sitting on the sidelines with Todd, Mike listened intently.

Ben squatted on his haunches as he slapped down a six of spades. "How come you know so much about what's going on, Harley?" he asked.

Harley spat to one side and wiped his mouth on his sleeve before he answered, "Nobody tells a foot soldier nothin', so a long time ago I learned to keep my ears open. That's how come I know what the officers talk about."

Ben grunted. "Well, if all they're gonna do is wait and try to make up their minds when they're gonna fight, I'll be long gone out of here, and so will the other volunteers who signed up with me. Our ninety days will be over on August fourteenth, some volunteers even earlier than that."

"Don't count on it," Harley answered. "If Lyon isn't goin' to get troops to replace the volunteers, then he's bound to go into action while he's still got men under contract." He studied his cards, then added, "Word is that Lyon's spies told him that the Rebs are movin' up strong from Cassville, hopin' to march on Springfield."

Mike couldn't help bursting in: "Then why doesn't General Lyon do something about it right now? General Sweeny sent those Rebs on the run down at Forsyth. We could do it again!"

Ben snickered. "Want to tell that to General Lyon, Harley?"

Harley laid down a card and smiled a satisfied smile. "I don't talk to generals. I listen to what they've got to say, and then I pass along the word."

But on August first, orders were given so swiftly that even Harley Botts had no advance notice. General Lyon had learned from his scouts that a strong column of Confederate soldiers was less than eighteen miles from Springfield.

That afternoon, the men in Major Sturgis's battalion left

camp and began their march to join Lyon's brigade. They forded Wilson's Creek, which was fairly shallow in the August heat, and halted in a field north of Skegg's Branch. Mike eagerly helped set up camp for nearly six thousand officers and men. He beat his drum calls with unmatched vigor and excitement, and the next morning, when the march began again, he was sure his drumbeats were the liveliest along the route.

Captain Steele, with a battalion and artillery, led the advance, chasing off a smattering of Confederates as he deployed two of his companies along Telegraph Road after them.

"I told you," Mike said proudly to Harley, as the march was halted and word was passed down the line, "it's easy to send those Rebs scurrying."

Harley grunted. "Don't be too sure. Take a look at what's around us—forest, thick underbrush, steep hills. It's easier to fight in the open than in terrain like this, take my word for it."

Word came that the Missouri State Guard had attacked Steele's vanguard at Dug Springs, so Lyon sent some of his brigade ahead to reinforce Steele's forces.

As instructed, Mike's company stood by to wait for further orders. "Why don't we go into action?" Mike demanded.

"Settle down," Todd answered. "We'll find out soon enough."

"Eager to fight, are you, boy?" Billy muttered.

To Mike's surprise, he saw that most of the men seemed restless or nervous. Few of them shared the excitement he felt.

That night at camp, rumors were as thick as the clouds of moths that beat against the lanterns' glass. A group of soldiers gathered around Harley, eager for any scrap of information, but Harley could only guess at what was happening.

8

THE NEXT MORNING, under cover of Totten's battery of guns, Lyon's army resumed its advance. Word filtered down that five men had died and thirty-six were wounded. Mike didn't know the men who'd been killed, so the statistics meant little to him. He was interested only in the order for the Second Kansas to advance past Dug Springs for three miles into McCulla's Springs, where the army would look for and engage the Confederates.

For twenty boring hours, the Second Kansas remained at McCulla's Springs, with no sign of a single gray-coated Reb, before Lyon recalled them. The general had heard that a large force of Confederates was moving to support General Sterling Price, and there was a strong chance that their cavalry would cut off Lyon's army from its base in Springfield, twenty-six miles to the northeast. To make matters worse, supplies were almost depleted.

"We're retreating? We've lost?" Mike was astounded when Harley passed on the news.

"We haven't lost," Harley explained. "We're just moving our army back a ways to regroup."

Mike must have looked as dismayed as he felt, because Harley said, "Have you ever played draughts—maybe chess?" When Mike nodded, Harley explained, "Pieces are moved here and there, back and forth, and it's called strategy."

"This isn't a game," Mike said stubbornly.

"No, it's war," Harley agreed. "But we've got to do what the general decides is best."

That night they camped at Terrell Creek, where the springs provided plenty of fresh water. Throughout the camp, soldiers supplemented their meager rations with boiled ears of newly ripened sweet corn from nearby fields.

The next day, Lyon led his army back to the outskirts of Springfield and ordered them to make a secure camp, allowing no one to leave or enter without proper credentials.

"He'd better have us do somethin' pretty soon," Ben complained. "It's gettin' closer and closer to August fourteenth."

"As I said before," Harley reminded him, "don't count on gettin' out by then. If Lyon loses most of his volunteers, he'll have to retreat practically out of the state and lose Missouri. Do you think he'll give up so easy?"

"I don't," Mike answered loyally, and went off to find Todd.

On August 8, a supply train arrived, providing many of the men with new clothes and shoes. Mike strode up and down in new, well-fitted boots, thankful he could throw away his old pair of shoes, which had large holes in the soles and one missing heel. Without the new boots, he'd probably have been marching south to meet the enemy in bare feet.

He chuckled to himself at the number of volunteers who complained about being issued "crooked shoes."

"Never had shoes like these afore this," Ben grumbled.

"One made for the right foot and one for the left. They're not as comfortable as the straight shoes I've always worn."

Mike had seen plenty of "straight shoes," shoes made with rounded toes to fit either foot. "Just be glad to have shoes," he said.

Mike knew they'd be either heading into battle or retreating from Missouri soon. Everyone had been expecting marching orders for days. On August 9, the orders came.

Soon after a dispatch from General Frémont, in which he stated his decision not to send reinforcements, one of Lyon's spies reported McCulloch's decision to attack the Federals on the following day.

Upon hearing this startling news, Lyon called for a council of war. Most of his officers agreed that retreating from Springfield would be a disaster. As Harley explained to the cluster of men around him, "The brigade would lose artillery and other equipment—and ultimately, the state of Missouri to the Confederacy."

"Surprise is our only hope," Lyon said. Captain Dawes informed his men of Lyon's decision to attack that very night.

Officers hurried to ready their troops to leave. Mike, his heart pounding, began to pack.

Sergeant Gridley looked at Mike's stuffed bedroll. "Leave it behind," he told Mike. "We have to travel as light as possible."

As Todd prepared to join Colonel Mitchell's unit, Mike gripped his hand. "Good luck," he said.

Todd's eyes were dark with fear. "Remember your promise," he said.

My promise? Oh, yes—the watch! "Of course I remember, but don't worry," Mike answered. "Just wish me good luck in return."

"Good luck, Mike," Todd murmured. He grabbed his bugle and ran to join the colonel.

He wouldn't be here except for my urging, Mike thought,

watching Todd go. But there was no time to think about it. The army was ready to move.

At six in the evening, with only two companies of home guards left to secure Springfield, the columns moved out. General Lyon's command, marching on the west flank along the Mt. Vernon Road, would cross Grand Prairie and attack the southerners' left flank. General Sigel took his troops to fight against the Confederates' rear and right.

The march began briskly, with some of the men singing loudly along with the drumbeat, Mike among them. The Kansas volunteers outsang them all as they bellowed "Happy Land of Canaan."

Close to midnight, Lyon ordered an end to the singing and drumming, as the noise might alert the enemy.

A little after one in the morning, Lyon's advance scouts discovered the Missouri State Guard's campfires and called a halt. The men rested, but only a few of them could sleep on the hard bare ground. Mike, his drum close to his side, found Todd by the moonlight's gleam on his bugle and squatted down next to him under a scrub oak. "It won't be long now," Mike said. "Those Rebs won't stand a chance."

"What time do you think we'll move in?" Todd asked.

"Probably not until light. It's too dark right now to know friend from foe."

Harley stumbled over a tree root, plopping down beside Mike and Todd. "If that don't beat all," he said. "I heard from Sergeant Gridley that yesterday two Rebel women spies, bold as brass but wrong as can be, got a pass to leave Springfield and drove down to talk to McCulloch at Wilson's Creek. Somehow they got the notion that General Lyon was packed up, ready to retreat from Springfield." He chuckled. "General Price, mad over the idea of the Federals gettin' away, told McCulloch he'd order the attack himself, if McCulloch wouldn't."

Todd asked, "The Rebs are going to attack *us*? When?"

Harley laughed again. "They were gonna start their

march about the same time we started ours, only they had a light rain shower, and McCulloch was afraid the rain would ruin his men's ammunition, which I understand is in short supply.

"Lyon's scouts discovered that the Confederates have withdrawn their pickets, thinkin' we turned tail, so they're set up for a surprise. In a few hours those Rebs will find out they don't need to come to us. We've already come to them!"

"How far away are the Rebs?" Mike asked.

"Less than three and a half miles," Harley answered. Grunting, he struggled to his feet. "You boys get your rest. You'll need it come morning."

As Harley left, Todd murmured, "I can't sleep. Can you?"

Mike sighed. "With all that's going on, how could anyone sleep?"

But in a few minutes Mike heard Todd's gentle snoring, and he leaned back against the tree trunk, staring up through the leafy branches at the smattering of bright stars.

The camp was nearly silent, with only the sounds of sleep and an occasional rustle of the underbrush traveling on the light breeze. Tears burned Mike's eyes as he thought of his family and the father he missed more than ever. "Da," he whispered, "I need you. Be with me now."

There was no answer, but Mike's mind and heart filled with contentment. Knowing that his father had heard him, he drifted off to sleep.

Suddenly, Mike started. Someone was shaking his shoulder. It took him several seconds to recognize Sergeant Gridley bending over him in the darkness.

"No call to *reveille* this morning, boys," the sergeant said. "It's four o'clock. Wake the men as quietly as you can."

As Mike and Todd scrambled to their feet, Todd murmured, "Remember your promise."

Shocked by the ghostly pallor of Todd's face, Mike said, "Todd, you know I will. But by this time tomorrow, we'll all be celebrating a big victory over those Rebs."

Without a word Todd snatched up his bugle and disappeared into the darkness.

Mike had no time to worry about his friend. He had work to do, and quickly.

By the time the night blue of the sky faded into a pearly pink-tinged gray, Lyon's battle line had been formed across the way from the northern end of the Confederate line. With infantry in front and Totten's battery just behind, the Union opened fire, and the Battle of Wilson's Creek began.

Eager to join the fray, Mike hurried to his post at Captain Dawes's side, only to discover that the Second Kansas was to be held in reserve, out of sight of the skirmish.

"Another wait! And for what?" Mike grumbled.

"What makes you so set on gettin' into the fight?" Ben mumbled close to Mike's ear. "It would suit me just fine if we stayed far and away from it."

"Stay out of the battle?" Mike was indignant. "Just what are you here for?"

Ben gave a long sigh. "Danged if I know. Right now I surely wish I'd stayed to home."

Mike listened to the booms of the cannons, the sharp blasts of gunfire, and the cries and shouts. Through the hubbub he could hear drum calls, and he squirmed impatiently as he clutched his own drum.

I'm a drummer, Mike thought restlessly. *I'm here, ready to serve. When am I going to get the chance?*

9

By the end of the first hour, the sounds of battle had grown to a head-pounding roar. The reserve army, most of whom were sprawled on the ground to get some rest, heard conflicting reports: The Rebs were putting up a vigorous battle. The Rebs were being beaten so badly, they'd never recover. The First Missouri and First Kansas had valiantly reached the site of what they were calling "Bloody Hill" and were winning the battle. If only that last report were true! No such luck. On the contrary, the shells from the Confederates' battery kept forcing back the Union troops.

By eight o'clock, Mike thought he couldn't stand to wait another minute. Then orders came for the Second Kansas to go to the aid of the First Missouri, which was about to be overcome. Colonel Mitchell, Captain Dawes, and the other officers mounted their horses.

It was close to nine o'clock and the sun was glaring a bright silver-gold, before Mike, energetically beating out the call to advance, began to climb the hill at Captain Dawes's

side. The men in Dawes's company eagerl
so Mike was almost upon the bodies that
the ground before he saw them. He gagged a
throat, and for an instant he was too sicken
drum.

"Steady, Mr. Kelly." Captain Dawes's voice

Mike took a deep breath and tried to concentrate on the drumbeats, but he couldn't ignore the sight of the dead all around him, some with gaping wounds in their chests, some with parts of their heads blown away. The most terrifying sight was the wounded soldiers who were still alive, some writhing and screaming in agony. No one at that moment could respond to their cries.

In desperation Mike forced his gaze beyond the crest of the hill to the cornfields and oatfields below, where men in blue fought men in gray, thrashing their way through the broken stalks. He noticed a small white farmhouse close to the road, not too far from Wilson's Creek. Confederate soldiers positioned at the back of the house kept up a barrage of fire at Union soldiers who had reached the roadway. Where were the people in the farmhouse? Mike wondered. Had they been able to get out of the way of this raging fury?

A bullet bounced off the rim of Mike's drum. The force made him stagger, but he quickly straightened, keeping his drumbeats loud and true despite the fear that knotted his stomach and made his head throb.

A wave of Rebs pushed forward, unloading their muskets. Then with no time to reload, they jabbed and stabbed all about them with the bayonets attached to the muskets' barrels.

A southerner about Todd's age bellowed in agony. He clasped a Union soldier who had fallen, screaming, "I shot my pa! Oh, God help me, I shot my pa!"

Horrified, Mike cried out, too, but what could his cries accomplish? A mass of Second Kansas volunteers rushed ward. After they had passed, the Reb lay dead on the ground next to his father.

Tears streamed down Mike's cheeks. As he hunched his shoulder to wipe them away, a blow from the side sent him sprawling.

It took Mike a moment to understand that a heavy body had fallen on top of him. As strong hands helped Mike to his feet, he looked at the face of the dead man.

"Captain Dawes!" he shouted. "No! Not the captain!"

Someone began leading Captain Dawes's horse away, the captain's body slung over the saddle. In a daze Mike staggered after them.

Sergeant Gridley grabbed Mike's shoulder and shoved the drumsticks into his hands. "Keep up the call to advance, Mr. Kelly. That's your job. I'll tell you if you need to drum *retreat*, and I hope that may never be."

"Y-yes, sir," Mike stammered. Sick at heart, cold with terror at the destruction all around him, Mike stood his post, his drumbeats steady.

Although Mike wouldn't have thought it possible, the fighting grew even more intense. The roar of the cannons, the musket fire, the screams and shouts . . . It was a bad dream, a bloodred nightmare, a horror that wouldn't end.

During a blessed lull in the fight, General Lyon rode up astride his gray horse and regrouped the Federal line. Leading the Second Kansas himself, Lyon began the charge against the Confederates, but the Rebs had rallied in even greater numbers, and the fighting grew fierce along the entire line.

For an hour the battle roared with fury. Mike, finding a perch on a rock ledge near the brow of the hill, bravely kept drumming. Nearby he could hear Todd's bugle. Mike could only hope the call to battle spurred the soldiers of his company onward, helping them to fight even more aggressively.

Near Mike a man cursed and nearly dropped his musket.

"The damned barrel's too hot!" he yelled. "It burnt my hands!"

A soldier at Mike's left fell. With an angry yell, Ben charged into the breach, cutting in front of Mike. But before he could shoot, an enemy bullet struck Ben's head, splattering his blood and brains onto Mike's face and jacket.

More powerful even than the wave of nausea that enveloped Mike was one horrible thought: He was alive only because Ben, brutally killed, had blocked a bullet aimed in his direction. As the battle raged around him, Mike beat his drum numbly, as though he were no longer a part of his own body.

A sudden burst of fire brought down General Lyon's horse. Lyon pulled himself out from under the animal and limped forward, waving his sword and shouting. Mike saw blood streaming from the general's forehead and his leg.

Soldiers from the First Iowa straggled back. "We have no leader!" someone shouted. "Give us a leader!"

"You have a leader," Mike heard Lyon call to them. "Sweeny, lead those troops forward. We will make one more charge!"

On his orderly's horse Lyon rode into the fray, swinging his hat and calling out to the Second Kansas, "Come on, my brave boys! I will lead you! Forward!"

His horse had taken but a few steps before Lyon clutched his chest and fell. His orderly caught him and carried him gently to the ground. "Our general is dead!" he cried.

The fierce blast of musket fire killed Colonel Mitchell, too. Many of the Union soldiers, dazed and confused, turned to retreat.

Mike slammed the drumsticks into their rat-tat-a-tat with all his strength. "This is not a call to retreat!" he shouted. "Fight, men! Fight the Rebs!"

Harley's strong voice bellowed, "Does the boy have

more spirit than the rest of us?" Harley ran ahead. The soldiers who had hesitated now turned and followed him.

"Good work, Mr. Kelly!" Sergeant Gridley called out, and Mike's eyes filled with tears. That was what Captain Dawes would have said. Mike's arms were heavy and painful from the relentless pounding of his drum. But beneath the mercilessly shining sun, Mike beat on.

Hearing the loud blare of Todd's bugle, Mike glanced to his right and saw Todd standing near the front lines.

"We'll beat them, Todd!" Mike yelled.

But before Todd could respond, Confederates surged toward the Federals. Whooping with excitement, a Reb charged directly at Todd, plunging his bayonet through Todd's chest.

"Todd! No! No!" Mike screamed, but there was nothing he could do.

Clutching his chest with a cry, blood spurting through his fingers, Todd fell to the ground and lay still.

With a grin the Reb scooped up Todd's bugle, tucked his trophy into his shirt, and plowed forward, holding his bayonet before him.

Mike started after the Reb who had killed Todd. "I'll get you!" he sobbed over and over.

But just as Mike stooped to pick up a musket, a horse rode into Mike's path. "Drummer!" the rider shouted. "Keep to your business! Sound *retreat*, boy! Now!"

Fighting nausea, tears streaming from his eyes, Mike obeyed orders. He dropped the musket and stood his ground, beating out the call, as the Rebs advanced with eager shouts.

Suddenly, a gray-uniformed Reb slammed through the underbrush and came face-to-face with Mike, his musket and bayonet pointed at Mike's forehead. Mike closed his eyes. This was it. He winced as he waited to be shot.

But the soldier groaned. "I can't shoot a boy!" he muttered.

The Reb roughly brushed past him, but there was no time for relief. Other Confederates were pouring up the hill and through the gap in the underbrush. A shot ripped through Mike's drum, tearing it from the strap around his neck, and another shot struck his right leg.

Mike fell from the ledge where he'd stood. He rolled uncontrollably down the hill, sharp pebbles scratching his face and arms. His leg felt as if it were on fire. *I have to get help or I'll die*, Mike thought. As he landed headfirst against a tree trunk, a sea of blackness curled around him, plunging him into a deep, pain-free unconsciousness.

10

Monster nightmares tortured Mike's dreams. He tried to cry out, but he couldn't. Through blinking eyes, he saw only darkness.

Don't fight the pain, Mike. Let go, he thought he heard Da say. With a sigh, Mike slipped into a blackness that soothed him like a stroking hand.

He awoke in a puddle of blood and sweat and mottled sunlight as a shower of pebbles stung his face. The sounds of war had vanished, leaving behind a silence even more horrible.

A few more pebbles rattled down the slope, striking Mike's face, and he glanced up through the noonday brightness to see a Confederate soldier making his way down the hill toward where he lay. The Reb yelled to someone out of Mike's sight, "There's a dead Yank down here! Looks like he's got fairly good boots. Ought to fit somebody."

"I don't like this robbin' the dead. That shouldn't be part

of a soldier's duty." The voice that had answered the Reb sounded familiar. Whose was it?

"We got their ammunition—what little was left—and you know the men in our company are in need of every pair of decent boots we can find."

"Long as we leave it at that," the familiar voice said. "But don't go through their pockets, Jiri. The bugle you been braggin' about should have been enough, but I saw you take that dead boy's pocket watch as well."

"It was mine by rights. I killed him."

Mike gasped and stiffened, remembering the grin on the Reb's face. Rage, stronger than his pain, poured like red-hot metal through Mike's mind and body, and he clenched his fists, biding his time.

"Besides, the watch won't do the Yank any good." The wiry blond Reb called Jiri laughed and slid farther down the bank until he stood next to Mike.

Mike's eyes narrowed to slits. As Jiri bent forward, Mike reached up and grabbed his neck, pulled Jiri off balance, and slammed his face into the dirt. Mike yelled, "Give me Todd's watch! Grave robber! Dirty Confederate grave robber!"

But Mike's wound had left him weak, and it took only a moment for Jiri to scramble free. He got to his feet and gave Mike a kick in the side. Mike cried out in pain.

Having reached the bottom of the slope, the other soldier grabbed Jiri and pulled him back just as he was aiming another kick.

"What's wrong with you, Jiri?" he shouted. "The man's wounded! For all we know, he's dyin'."

"He attacked me!" Jiri complained.

"He stole Todd's watch!" Yelling the words took all Mike's energy.

Grinning, Jiri pulled the watch from his pocket and dangled it out of Mike's reach. "It's mine now," he said. "I got it fair and square off a dead Yank."

The watch had baby tooth marks on it. There was no doubt about it—the watch was Todd's.

The other soldier shoved Jiri aside and stared down at Mike. "Well, I'll be!" he said. "It's you, Mike Kelly."

Mike looked into the eyes of the tall lean Reb with sun-bleached hair and gasped. "Corey Blair!" he cried out. Mike well remembered Corey, who had been so intent on courting and marrying Marta, the young woman who worked for Mike's first adoptive parents, Mr. and Mrs. Friedrich.

"If you can, get up and come with us," Corey said.

"As a prisoner," Jiri sneered.

"I can't get up," Mike told Corey. "My leg . . ."

Corey tore Mike's pants leg free from the wound. He made a retching sound. "Looks awful," he said, and turned back toward Mike, his face pale. He wiped at the sweat on his forehead. "Mike, you got hurt bad and lost a lot of blood. There's pus and dirt and maggots in the wound."

"I'm not going to die," Mike said firmly.

Corey managed a shaky grin. "I'll go along with that. A nearly dead man couldn't pull Jiri off his feet the way you done."

As if he'd just remembered Jiri, Corey stood and said to the other man, "Why don't you go see what else you can find? I'll take care of this one."

"He's a Yank. Why not just shoot him in the head?"

Corey flushed. "I'd as soon shoot *you* as him. The battle's over, and the Federals have been gone since yesterday."

"Leaving us to bury their dead," Jiri grumbled.

"It makes no nevermind," Corey told him. "This man is our prisoner, and we don't shoot prisoners."

Jiri glanced at Mike's leg. "He'll probably beg you to shoot him after he finds out the surgeon's gonna take off his leg."

Mike's heart raced. "Corey? Your surgeon wouldn't do that, would he?"

With a nasty laugh, Jiri began to climb the slope, and Corey bent to study Mike's leg. This time Mike could feel him pushing and probing around the wound. Mike bit his lip to keep from crying out. When Corey finished, Mike fell back, exhausted.

"The bone's not broke," Corey said. "As far as the wound goes, it's stopped bleedin', and it needs a good cleanin' out. 'Course, I'm no company surgeon, and like Jiri said, the doctor we got is kinda inclined to handle bad leg wounds by taking off the leg."

Mike clutched at Corey's hand. "Don't let him cut off my leg! Please, Corey! Let me just stay here until I've got my strength back."

"You lie here much longer in this heat, with those maggots eatin' away at that wound, and there won't be anything left of you."

"But my leg—"

"Listen to me, Mike," Corey said. "I've got to take you to where you'll get care."

"Then take me to my own company."

"No chance in the world for that. Your Federals were retreatin' fast. By this time, they've reached Springfield and then some. With our army on their tail, they'll have to keep movin'. No telling where they'll run to."

Without Todd. Without me. The last bit of Mike's resolve melted, and he burst into tears.

Corey was silent for a few moments, then touched Mike's shoulder. "You're no older than my brother Ezra. I don't know what gave you the notion to join the army, but you did, so you gotta get yourself in hand now. You done me some favors by carryin' my notes to Marta, so I promise I'll see you get care, Mike, and I'll do whatever I can to keep you from losin' your leg."

Mike struggled to get himself under control. He rubbed the tears from his eyes with the back of one hand and looked up at Corey. "Thanks, Corey," he said.

Corey's smile was brief. "I'm gonna have to carry you up this slope and out of here," he said. "I won't try to fool you, Mike. Afore I get you to the hospital that's been set up at the farmhouse, your leg's gonna hurt somethin' awful."

Mike nodded. "I understand."

"Okay," Corey said. "Reach up and grab me around the neck."

Mike did, and Corey swung him upward and over one shoulder.

"Don't worry if you can't hang on," Corey said. "I've got a good hold on you."

Pain streaked through Mike's entire body. This time he didn't try to fight it. Gratefully, he slipped back into the darkness.

Mike awoke to find himself lying on the ground in the shade of the white farmhouse he'd spotted from the ridge on the hill. Around him were other wounded men. Some lay still, eyes closed, wrapped in blankets, while others cried out in agony. A man crawled over Mike's feet. "Oooh!" Mike yelled, but the man didn't hear. Moaning, talking to himself in delirium, he crawled on, sprawling over the bloody blanket of the man who lay next to Mike.

"Did he hurt you?" Mike asked as he twisted toward the injured soldier.

The man didn't answer. His half-lidded eyes were dull, his jaw slack. The soldier was dead.

An officer, his clothes stained with blood, approached the row of wounded where Mike lay. Following the officer was an orderly with a sheaf of papers on which were printed large numbers. As the officer examined each injured man, he spoke to the orderly, and the orderly tied one of the papers to each one's coat buttons.

This must be the company surgeon, Mike thought, and he was so frightened, he found it hard to breathe.

The doctor spent only a moment looking at Mike's

wound. "Infection's already set in," he said to the orderly. "We'll have to cut it off."

"No!" Mike yelled.

The doctor took a good look at Mike and the grubby clothes he was wearing. "A Yank, are you? Well, sorry, son, but it's the best we can do for you. Most of the men injured here will soon die of infection. Wouldn't you rather give up your leg and save your life?"

Mike struggled to regain his composure so he could tell the doctor that the bones in the leg weren't broken and that he was sure the wound could heal with proper care, but the officer didn't wait for an answer. "Remove the dead man for burial," he instructed. An instant later, he began examining the next patient.

As a group of soldiers approached, Mike stiffened. He'd put up a fight, he would! No one was going to cut off his leg!

But while two of the soldiers picked up the dead man, it was Corey who bent over Mike.

"Close your eyes," Corey whispered. "Let your jaw drop, and whatever you do, don't let anybody see you breathe!"

Corey shouted to another soldier in the detail, "This one died on us, too. He's small enough. I'll carry him myself."

Despite his terrible pain, Mike didn't flinch as Corey moved him. He hung limply in Corey's arms, until they had left the farmhouse far behind and entered a cool grove of trees. Mike could hear water lapping and splashing over rocks nearby.

Barely opening his eyes, Mike glimpsed a sturdy, middle-aged woman standing by the bank of the wide creek, waiting for them.

"Where are we? What are you doing?" Mike whispered to Corey.

Corey gently put Mike down next to the creek bank. "Miz Ray, this is my friend Mike I told you about," he said. "Mike, this is the lady whose family lives in the white farmhouse." Corey turned back to Mrs. Ray. "The surgeon wants to take

Mike's leg, but he's just a boy. What do you think? Will the infection kill him, or could we save his leg?"

Mike stared off in the distance as Mrs. Ray knelt beside him and examined his leg. The answer would depend on this woman.

"Mike," Mrs. Ray finally told him, "look at me." When he did, she asked, "How old are you, son?"

"Close to thirteen," he answered truthfully.

Mrs. Ray sighed. "I've got a boy who'll soon be your age." She paused, then looked up at Corey. "I've seen wounds worse than this heal, with the right kind of care. I'll take him into the house and put him in John Wesley's bed. But first we've got to get Mike clean. I've brought kerosene for the lice in his hair, strong lye soap and a brush to get rid of the dirt, and alcohol to cleanse the wound, once the rest is accomplished. Will you remove his clothes, please?"

"Ma'am!" Mike gasped. "You can't! I mean, *I* can't! That is—"

"Nonsense," Mrs. Ray said. "I'm a mother, and I'm going to be your nurse. I don't think you want us to take you back to the surgeon, Mike."

"No," Mike whispered, but he squeezed his eyes shut and burned with embarrassment.

"We'll be as gentle as we can, Michael, but there will be some pain, and you'll have to be brave." She took his hand. "I would rather no one from the army detachment knew we were here."

Mike just nodded. He didn't—couldn't—open his eyes.

The acrid smells of kerosene and soap he could stand. He didn't even mind when Mrs. Ray scrubbed his skin until it seemed to be on fire. But when she began to clean his wound, he had to shove his fist into his mouth and bite his knuckles to keep from crying out.

Finally, when Mike thought he couldn't stand the pain another minute, Mrs. Ray murmured, "You're a good boy,

Mike," and began to wrap his leg tightly with strips of clean white cloth.

Corey slipped a soft nightshirt over Mike's head, awkwardly trying to poke Mike's hands and arms into the sleeves. Finally, Corey once again lifted him in his arms.

"Now," Mrs. Ray said in a businesslike manner as she picked up her tools, "what you need, Mike, is sleep."

"I have to rejoin my company," Mike said. "I have to report."

"Not until you're well enough to travel," Mrs. Ray said firmly. "Come along, Corey. We'll put Mike to bed."

As they approached the Rays' farmhouse, Mike could see across the valley to the crushed stalks of the cornfields, where a detail of Confederates were collecting and burying the dead bodies of men from both armies. The dead horses remained, for now, sprawled out in the fields, their stinking, decaying flesh swelling in the heat.

As they silently passed through the yard and entered the house, Mike flinched at the moans of the wounded men who covered the nearby ground and the Rays' front porch.

Corey brought Mike to an upstairs bedroom. The bed—one of four in the room—was soft and clean, and Mike sank into it gratefully. "Thanks, Mrs. Ray. Thanks, Corey," he murmured. But his head still throbbed, and his leg still ached. Even sleep failed to relieve his pain. In his dreams he was burning. He cried out for Todd, he called for Ma.

"He isn't going to live through the fever," he heard a woman say.

But Mrs. Ray answered, "We'll do our best."

Hands bathed him with water so cold that Mike shook. For a short while the heat slipped away, and he slept. But before long the feverish pain swept through his body again. "Ma! Help me, Ma," Mike murmured. The cooling hands bathed him again and again.

The fiery dreams slowly trailed away, like smoke from a long smoldering campfire, and Mike awoke to find a tall black woman cradling his shoulders. She smiled and lifted him into a sitting position, then held a spoonful of broth to his mouth. "Mrs. Ray says it's time to get some nourishment into you."

"The battle," Mike mumbled, for that was all he could remember. Where was he now? And who was Mrs. Ray? "Yesterday . . ."

"It wasn't yesterday," the woman said with a chuckle. "It's been near a week since you got here."

"I had fever." Mike shuddered as he remembered his dreams.

"Yes, you did, Michael. I, for one, didn't think you'd survive, but Mrs. Ray is a good nurse. She brought you through it."

Mike sighed as the full memory of what had happened came back to him. "I'm tired," he said. "I just want to sleep."

"Eat the soup, and I'll let you go back to sleep."

Mike obediently gulped the broth from the spoon she held to his lips. When the bowl was empty, the woman gently laid Mike back against the pillows. "Thank you," he said, "Mrs. . . . Miss . . . ?"

"I'm called Aunt Rhoda," she said with a smile, and plumped Mike's pillows.

He looked up at her. "Are you a slave?"

"Never mind about that now," she said. She smoothed Mike's blanket with one hand while she balanced his soup bowl and spoon with the other.

"Are the Rays southern sympathizers?" he asked.

Aunt Rhoda was firm. "The Rays are Federal. They have to be because Mr. Ray is the postmaster for these parts. He'd lose his job if he wasn't Federal."

"How can they be Federal and still have slaves?"

"Hush, now. It's best for you if you get some sleep."

But Mike couldn't give up. "You could be free in Kansas."

"Kansas?" Aunt Rhoda shook her head as she walked to the door, where she paused to look at Mike. "Me and my husband Wiley and our four children live in a nice little house behind the Rays' farmhouse. Maybe sometime, when this war is over, we'll be free, but we've got no cause to leave here—especially now, when no one knows what's gonna happen next."

"Aunt Rhoda . . ." Mike began, but she had shut the door.

Weariness overcame him, and he settled back against the pillows, immediately falling asleep. He dreamed of Todd as he had laughed and conspired with Mike to run away and join the Union Army. In the dream Todd's mother was calling her son's name, over and over again. "Answer her," Todd told Mike. "She doesn't know that I can't." Mike tried, but he couldn't form the words. The sounds that came from his mouth were sobs, and Mike awoke to find that his pillow was wet.

During the late afternoon, Mike occasionally heard the creak of the bedroom door opening. He'd open his eyes in time to see a face peeking in at him and quickly disappearing. Each face was different. How many children did Mr. and Mrs. Ray have?

A boy entered the bedroom, firmly shutting the door behind him. "I'm John Wesley," he said. "I'm supposed to help you with the chamber pot." He slid the pot out from its place under the bed.

Mike's face grew hot. "I can do it myself," he said. But as he tried to climb out of bed, a strong wave of pain pushed him back against the pillows.

"Around here we do what Ma says whether we like it or not." John Wesley made a face as he proceeded to help Mike. "You don't look old enough to be in the army," he said. "Did you carry a gun? Did you shoot any Confederate soldiers?"

"I'm not old enough to be a soldier," Mike admitted. "I'm a drummer—a company musician." He pulled the blanket up and tried to ignore the chamber pot, upon which John Wesley had slapped a lid, ready to take it outside to empty.

"I know that drummers have an important job in relaying orders to the soldiers," John Wesley said. "Pa told me. And he told me that drummers get shot at just like regular soldiers."

"That's what happened to me," Mike said.

John Wesley studied Mike with respect. "You have to be very brave to be a drummer."

Mike didn't answer. There was a time—it seemed like years and years ago—that he'd thought he was very brave. But he'd never been so scared in his whole life as when he went into battle.

A firm voice called from downstairs, "John Wesley Ray! What's keeping you?"

"I'll be back later," John Wesley said. He hurried out, leaving the door ajar.

Mike lay back against his pillows, deliberately and painfully reviewing the battle in his mind. Captain Dawes had been killed, as had Ben, but what about Sergeant Gridley? And Harley? And Billy? Mike could see the faces of some of the other men in his company. What had happened to them? Where were they now?

A man's gruff voice, coming from somewhere downstairs, broke into his thoughts: "Ma'am, I've heard that you're harborin' a Union soldier under your roof."

Mrs. Ray's voice was every bit as firm and clear. "Whether we are or not makes no difference, Captain. Your General McCulloch issued an order that said that prisoners would be released and allowed to return to their friends."

"That order is about to be countermanded, ma'am. General Price has a different idea about prisoners, and he's about to issue a statement to the populace of Missouri." After a pause and a rustle of paper, the captain said, "Here . . . I'll read you that part." Raising his voice, he continued, " 'I warn all evil-disposed persons, who may support the usurpations of anyone claiming to be provisional or temporary governor of Missouri, or who shall in any other way give aid or comfort to the enemy, that they will be held as enemies, and treated accordingly.' And now, ma'am, with or without your permission, I'm going upstairs to see if you're hiding a Yankee soldier."

Mike clutched the edge of the blanket, barely able to breathe, as he heard the officer's heavy footsteps thumping up the stairs.

11

As the captain appeared in the doorway, children of all ages scooted in and around him. Some of the children were almost as tall as the captain, some barely higher than his knees. Mike stared, wide-eyed.

John Wesley pushed to the forefront. "Don't worry," he said to the captain. "We don't think our brother's contagious."

"Contagious?" The captain hesitated.

Rolling his eyes, John Wesley lowered his voice to almost a whisper. "And we're almost sure it isn't smallpox."

John Wesley crossed his eyes and began scratching his arms and chest. Two of the smaller children immediately copied him. The captain nervously backed away from the doorway, bumping into Mrs. Ray, who had just joined the group. "Has the company doctor seen your son who's ill, ma'am?" he asked.

"My son?" Mrs. Ray's eyes widened, but she quickly recovered. "As you can see, your company doctor has his hands full. Michael is recuperating and will soon be well."

One of the younger children stepped on the captain's toes as she shoved her way out the door. Pain lined his face as he dodged her path. "How many children do you have, ma'am?" he asked Mrs. Ray.

"Mr. Ray and I have been blessed with quite a large family," Mrs. Ray said. She put her hand to the forehead of a little girl who was scratching vigorously. "What's the matter, Livonia?" she asked. "Are you not feeling well?"

"Mrs. Ray," the captain told her, "I would like to search the rest of your house."

"Do whatever you must do," Mrs. Ray answered. "The children will accompany you."

"That's not necessary," the captain barked, and his footsteps beat a swift tattoo as he strode down the hallway, most of the children on his heels.

John Wesley looked up at his mother. "I wasn't fibbing—well, not exactly."

Smiling, Mrs. Ray put a hand on her son's shoulder, then turned to Mike. "Mr. Ray and I have taught our children that when a law is terribly unjust, then it is wrong to obey it," she said. "To take you as a prisoner at this time, Mike, would surely mean your death."

"Thank you, Mrs. Ray," Mike mumbled.

Yet he wondered: Mrs. Ray was a good, kind woman who taught her children to be just—yet she owned slaves. How could anyone believe that slavery was just?

"Sleep well," Mrs. Ray said. "Most of the troops have gone north to occupy Springfield. The others will soon leave. You're a part of our family for the present. You'll be safe here with us."

But it wasn't long before Mike had another visitor. Corey came to Mike's bedside and smiled down at him. "You look a lot better than you did, Mike Kelly."

"Thanks to you," Mike said.

"And to Mrs. Ray. She'll take good care of you."

"Do you know what happened to my company? Where they went?" Mike asked.

Corey shrugged. "Last I heard, your Major Sturgis was still leading his army northeast. Someone said the Yanks were headed for Rolla, as far as they could get from us Confederates." He blustered a bit as he added, "They may have to run all the way to St. Louis."

Mike didn't want to hear Corey brag about the Union Army's defeat. Besides, there was something important he had to discuss with Corey. "Your friend Jiri—" Mike began, but Corey interrupted.

"Jiri Logan's no friend of mine."

Mike got right to the point. "He stole my friend's pocket watch."

"I know that," Corey answered.

When Corey didn't say anything else, Mike burst out, "Todd's father gave him that watch, and Todd wanted it to go to his sister Emily, if he was killed. I promised to take it to her. Jiri has to give me the watch!"

"No, he doesn't. Jiri took the watch off one of the enemy. Sorry—off your friend. If Jiri hadn't taken the watch, somebody else would have. You didn't see, but all the camp followers were goin' through the pockets of the dead and wounded."

"Corey," Mike insisted, "I've got to get that watch." *And I've got to get Jiri*, he thought, fighting to control his rage.

"You're in no shape to take it away from him." Corey couldn't help smiling. "And I'm not about to get in the middle of a fight over a plain ol' watch that could be bought in any general store in Missouri, so don't ask me to do the job for you."

Mike exploded, "It's not fair!"

"Who said war was fair?" Corey reached down to give a rough pat to Mike's shoulder. "Good-bye, Mike Kelly. I hope we never meet up on a battlefield again."

"Where are you off to?" Mike asked.

"Springfield, to Sterling Price's outfit."

Good, Mike thought. Now he knew where he could find Jiri.

Corey grinned, as though he could tell what Mike was thinking. "When I next see Marta," he said, "I'll tell her you haven't changed a bit and are still as aggrivatin' as any little red-topped bantam rooster."

Mike managed to smile in return. "Good luck, Corey."

Funny, Mike thought as Corey left. He had just wished good luck to a Confederate soldier who'd soon be in combat against Mike's own army. Well, it was no crazier than Federal sympathizers owning slaves, or generals countermanding each other's orders, or fathers and sons on opposite sides. Mike shut his eyes, recalling the two men, young and old, who lay dead in each other's arms, father in blue and son in gray.

His head hurt, and his eyes were too heavy to open again. He burrowed into the pillow and once again escaped into sleep.

Mike wrote to all his family, but he didn't describe the battle. He wrote simply that he'd been wounded, that Mrs. Ray and her family were taking good care of him, and that he'd soon be rejoining his company. They could write to him at his army address.

The last of the Confederate troops had left the area, so Mike didn't worry that he might be discovered and taken prisoner. What bothered him was that there was no way to get word to his own company that he was alive.

Over the next few weeks Mike didn't lack for visitors. Even at night he had company. The Ray boys piled into the other beds in Mike's room, and John Wesley slept on a pallet on the floor. The room was filled with the gentle snores and whistles of heavy sleepers. All was peaceful until Mike shouted through his nightmares, waking the other boys, who grumbled in frustration. Mike never told them that the memories of battle that haunted him by day were even worse than those in his dreams. What had become of Harley and Billy and Sergeant Gridley? Mike was afraid to find out.

Some of the younger Ray children were steady visitors to Mike's room, and each of them described their fright on that horrible August day.

Olivia shook her head until her dark brown curls bounced. "Wesley and Livonia and me were herdin' our horses in the valley south of the spring house when, all of a sudden, up rode a Confederate soldier, scarin' us half to death."

John Wesley interrupted. "He yelled to us to get out of there and said, 'There's gonna be fightin' like hell in less than ten minutes.' "

Livonia gasped and murmured, "Ma said you weren't to say that word ever again, Wesley."

Looking smug, John Wesley answered, "I'm just telling Mike exactly what the soldier said, that's all."

"Well, be quiet because it's my turn now," Livonia announced. "Everybody—even Aunt Rhoda and Wiley and their children and Mr. Short, the postman who works for Pa—all of us hid in the cellar for hours and hours with nothin' to eat but a pan of biscuits Ma scooped up when she ran through the kitchen."

"There was fightin' all around us!" Olivia said. "We had to stay in the cellar until the battle was over."

"Not all of us," John Wesley broke in. "Ma and Aunt Rhoda went outside to tend the wounded when they heard the soldiers being brought to the house."

"Then as soon as the fightin' was over and Federal prisoners were taken, Pa was made to help escort the prisoners to Springfield," Olivia said. "He had to walk there and back—over twenty-five miles each way—because the Confederates stole all our horses."

"One of the Rebs stole my friend's pocket watch," Mike

muttered. He told the children the story, fighting to keep his voice steady as he spoke of Todd.

"Now Emily will never have her brother's watch," Livonia said sadly.

"It's not right!" Olivia added.

But John Wesley quizzically raised one eyebrow and lowered his voice. "If I was you, Mike, I'd go find that polecat Jiri Logan and sneak in his tent after it got dark and snatch the watch back."

Mike nodded. He could see himself slinking noiselessly like a dark shadow to the place where Jiri slept, searching for the watch, finding it easily, and slipping it into his own pocket. Why not? Hadn't Da himself insisted that nothing was impossible to accomplish if you put your mind to it? And then . . . if he had a knife or a gun . . .

He gasped, shaken at his strong desire to kill Jiri. *It was like running to the edge of a precipice,* Mike thought. He had come so close to planning Jiri's murder. . . . To kill an enemy during battle would be one thing, but to take a life in revenge would be nothing more than murder. Did he really hate enough to murder?

"No," Mike whispered.

"No?" John Wesley looked surprised. "You aren't going after your friend's watch?"

"The watch, yes," Mike answered. "I am."

"Then why did you say no?"

"Never mind, John Wesley. The point is, I *am* going after the watch."

John Wesley's eyes grew wide with excitement, but Olivia announced, "That's a stupid idea. It's far too dangerous."

Livonia hopped from her perch on the end of the bed, a self-righteous look on her face. "I'm gonna tell Ma." She ran from the room.

Olivia ran after her.

Mike wasn't worried. Mrs. Ray would put the story down

as a childish fancy. After all, he walked with a limp. He'd grown pale and had lost weight. He looked a long stretch from being able to take on a man as full of good health and energy as Jiri Logan. But Mike knew that with careful planning he could work out a way. In the meantime, he'd help Mr. Ray sort the mail in the post office he'd set up in a front room.

The few people who came to the house from neighboring farms assumed that Mike—who dressed in hand-me-downs from Mrs. Ray's older boys—was a recuperating Confederate soldier, and for Mike's protection and their own, the Rays allowed them to think so. The visitors were full of information—both true and exaggerated—about conflicts throughout the State of Missouri and the comings and goings of the Union and Confederate armies.

Mike was especially interested in the news from John Greene, one of the Rays' neighbors on Wire Road. It was he who reported that Confederate generals McCulloch and Pearce had returned to Fort Smith, Arkansas, while General Sterling Price had resumed his command over the Missouri State Guard and marched his men north to Lexington, a town high on the bluffs overlooking the Missouri River. He was poised for attack.

On August 30, Greene scowled as he announced, "That Federal fool, Major General John Frémont, proclaimed martial law, ordered an automatic death sentence for guerrilla fighters, and stated that all slaves owned by Confederates in Missouri are now free."

Mike looked toward the kitchen where Aunt Rhoda was stirring a batch of biscuits for supper. She had paused for just a moment. Had she heard the news she was free?

"I wonder, what is that going to mean for Missouri?" Mr. Ray asked.

"It'll mean exactly nothing." Greene's scowl turned to a chuckle. "Speakin' rash won't do Frémont any good with the President. Do you think he wants to lose all those slaveholders to the Confederate side?"

On September 20, Greene crowed, "Frémont had enough good sense to pull the army out of Springfield and back to Rolla."

"Who holds Springfield now?" Mr. Ray asked.

"General Sterling Price," Greene answered proudly. "Price's army overcame the Union garrison. How about that? Another Confederate victory!"

Mike shuddered as he remembered how Harley compared the moves on a chessboard with the moves of armies at war. War wasn't a game. It was pure horror. He'd testify to that at any time, any place.

Mike had been a guest of the Rays for over a month and a half when he decided he couldn't stay a moment longer. Although his leg still ached and he walked with a limp, he couldn't remain inactive while the war raged on. Mike told Mr. and Mrs. Ray it was time he went back to his outfit.

"Oh, Mike, another few weeks . . ." Mrs. Ray pleaded.

"Mike's well on the mend," Mr. Ray countered. "If he feels it's time to go, then we'll do what we can to help him reach Rolla." His forehead puckered. "I wish I had a horse to give you, Mike."

"I know the Rebs took all your horses," Mike said.

Mr. Ray sighed. "Who knows when they may return and take the two I bought last week?" For a moment his eyes darkened, but he quickly continued, "One of our near neighbors, Marcus Peebles, is driving a wagonload of corn to market in Springfield tomorrow. He can give you a lift that far, and if you avoid whatever Confederates are camped outside of Springfield, you might be lucky enough to get a ride from someone going on to Rolla."

Mike could hardly contain himself as John Wesley, acting as messenger, rode one of the horses to Marcus Peebles's house. To Mike's delight, Mr. Peebles sent back word for Mike to meet him at six the next morning in front of the Ray house on the Wire Road, which they'd follow into Springfield.

Mrs. Ray brought Mike his uniform, washed, mended, and folded, the jaunty forage cap resting on top. "For when you're finally back with your company," she said.

Mike rolled the clothes so that they could be tied into a makeshift pack. John Wesley brought him a waterproof knapsack to put them in, along with the change of drawers and socks that his ma had put on the bed. The next morning the whole Ray family was up to give Mike a good send-off.

Mike was embarrassed by the hugs from the girls, but he wrapped his arms tightly around Mrs. Ray. "I'll always be in debt to you. You saved my life," he said.

"Safe journey to you, Mike," Mrs. Ray whispered, tears in her eyes. "I pray you'll soon return home safely to your family."

Mike hugged Aunt Rhoda, who gave him an encouraging smile. "You listen to Mrs. Ray, Mike. Soon as your three months are up, you get along home. The army's no place for a growing boy."

"Mike," John Wesley whispered eagerly, pulling him aside, "what are you gonna do about your friend's watch? If Jiri Logan's camped near Springfield, will you try to get the watch away from him?"

"I don't know yet how I'll manage it," Mike answered, clenching his fists in determination, "but Jiri isn't going to end up with that watch. Emily Blakely is!"

As Mike climbed up to the seat of Marcus Peebles's wagon, he fought back the fear that sat in his stomach like a ball of lead. Jiri Logan was tall and wiry and strong. What chance in the world would Mike have to keep his dangerous promise?

12

MIKE SOON FOUND that Mr. Peebles wasn't a talkative man. To be sure, he had much to grumble about: both of the armies, which were trampling down fields that meant a family's livelihood; "Old Ape," who had caused all the problems with his presidential busybodying; and the miserable September heat. Otherwise, Mr. Peebles rode in silence, definitely not going out of his way to enliven the trip.

But as they approached Springfield, with the Confederate camp ahead of them, Mike tensed, gripping the edge of the wooden seat.

Mr. Peebles studied Mike from the corner of his eye. "That eager to get back to duty? . . . Or are you?"

"What do you mean?" Mike asked.

"Heard you were a drummer for the Confederates. Isn't that right?"

Mike tried to sound calm. "I think my division's moved on north. I'll ride with you into town."

"Won't know for sure, less'n you stop at the camp and ask," Mr. Peebles said.

"I can ask in town."

Mr. Peebles studied Mike through narrowed eyes. "You ain't a deserter, are you?"

"No!" Mike snapped.

"Don't take my head off. It's a fair question. 'Specially for someone who seems bent on avoidin' the Confederate camp."

Mike bit his lip as he desperately tried to think of what to do.

As they approached the road to the camp, where a traffic of Confederate soldiers, sutlers, and camp visitors were moving in and out of the gate, Mr. Peebles tugged at the reins, stopping his wagon. Two soldiers crossed the road in front of the wagon, and Mr. Peebles called out, "Boy here wants to rejoin his division! Where does he go to find out where they're located?"

"Whose division is he looking for?" the shorter, stockier soldier asked, as both of them examined Mike with a look of surprise.

With as much bounce and energy as his aching leg would allow him, Mike snatched up his knapsack and jumped from the wagon seat. Luck was with him—the badges they wore were the same as the one on Corey's uniform. Mike smiled and called out, "Well now, men, judging from the fine look and fit of the both of you, this must be the Missouri State Guard."

Both soldiers laughed, and Mike began walking with them toward the gate, turning just once to wave his thanks to Mr. Peebles. Satisfied, Mr. Peebles clucked to his horses, flipped the reins, and took off down the road toward Springfield.

"Are you telling us the Guard's stooped to hiring children?" one of the men teased Mike.

Mike grinned. "That fellow driving the wagon needs either his eyes or his head examined. Imagine his thinking I'm a Confederate soldier—a lad who's not yet reached his thirteenth year!"

The soldiers chuckled, but one of them asked, "If you're not with the Guard, then what business do you have here at camp?"

Mike was prepared for the question. "I've got a good friend with the Guard, Corey Blair, and before I'm off and away to who knows where, I'd like to say good-bye to him. Do either of you know Corey?"

The taller man nodded. "I know him, but I'm not sure he's here in Springfield. Scouting details were sent east and north. Corey may have gone with either of them."

"Jiri Logan, as well?"

The soldier glanced at Mike sharply. "My advice is for you to have as little to do with Jiri Logan as possible."

The other man smiled. "Pay no mind to whatever this sour-face tells you. His gambling losses have clouded his mind."

"Logan cheated!"

"It was only your word against his."

"Logan's too blamed clever. I couldn't prove what he'd done."

"Then why get in a card game with him? You might as well throw your pay in the ditch."

As the soldiers argued, Mike thought about the choices before him. There seemed to be thousands of Rebs in the camp. What chance would he have if one of them found him out? But Jiri Logan might be right here under his nose. For Todd's sake, Mike had to get into that camp and retrieve the watch.

Security at the gate was lax, and no one challenged Mike as he limped into the encampment. He kept his eyes open. If Corey or Jiri spotted him, he was as good as dead. Trying not to let his voice betray his pounding heart, Mike began to ask a few of the soldiers if they knew where he might find Logan.

Most soldiers just shrugged, but one finally directed him to the last row of tents near the north side of the encampment. "Fifth one down, I think, although I doubt he'd be there this time of day."

All the better, Mike thought. Jiri wasn't likely to have the watch, or any other belongings he'd stolen, on his person. They'd be hidden away—maybe in a blanket roll.

The tent area wasn't as busy as the rest of the camp. Mike was alone as he limped down the last row to the fifth tent. Holding his breath, he stopped and listened. There were no sounds coming from inside the tent. Cautiously, he lifted a corner of the flap that served as a door and peered inside.

Good! It was empty!

Mike slipped from the bright sunshine into the tent, where he saw neat piles of bedrolls and equipment—enough for at least four men.

The watch could well be in one of these knapsacks, Mike thought, bending toward the knapsack on his right. But before he could begin his search, strong arms circled him and roughly jerked him off his feet. Gasping, he sailed through the air and fell with a plop onto the hard-packed dirt outside the tent. Dizzy from pain, Mike grabbed his sore leg and fought the tears that blurred his vision.

Fists at his waist, a red-faced sergeant glared down at Mike and growled, "You're up to no good, I can tell. What are you after in my tent, boy?"

Mike flinched and wiped his eyes on his sleeve. "I thought it was Jiri Logan's tent. I'm looking for him."

"Why?"

"Why? Well, uh—to say hello," Mike stammered. "I heard he was here."

"You heard wrong. His battalion left the camp last week for Rolla." The sergeant squinted as he studied Mike from head to toe. Finally, he said, "Turn out the contents of your knapsack."

His knapsack! The sergeant would discover Mike's Union Army uniform, and he'd be thought a spy. Spies were hanged.

Mike shivered as a chill passed through him. What if he never saw his family again—not even to say good-bye? His resolve to be brave couldn't stop the tears from flooding his eyes and rolling down his cheeks. "I'm not a thief," he insisted.

The sergeant cleared his throat and awkwardly shifted his weight from one foot to the other. "S-stop that bawling," he said uncomfortably. "Are you a man, or aren't you?"

Well, Mike thought. His tears seemed to be coming in handy. He allowed a few more sobs to escape. "You can see I'm not a man," he said. "I'm not yet thirteen."

As Mike continued to snuffle, the sergeant's gaze shifted nervously from side to side. "No more of that!" he ordered. "Anyone who heard and saw you would think I'd been giving you a beating."

Mike wailed and raised his hands protectively over his head. "Don't hit me!" he cried.

The sergeant took a step back. "Get out of here, you young rapscallion!" he demanded. "Start running now, and don't stop until you reach Springfield! Do you hear me?"

"Yes, sir!" Mike scrambled to his feet and clutched his knapsack tightly, hobbling as fast as he could until he knew the sergeant could no longer see him. After a quick stop to catch his breath and rub his painful leg, Mike passed the sentries at the gate and headed once again for Springfield.

That escape had been much too close. Suppose the uniform had been discovered? As he limped along, Mike went over and over what had happened. He'd taken too much of a chance, entering the tent in broad daylight. He wouldn't make a serious mistake like that again. He also knew that it would be a lot safer not to have a Union Army uniform in his possession while he was traveling through Confederate-occupied territory.

Mike sighed with frustration. No matter what the danger, he couldn't—he *wouldn't*—ditch the uniform of which he was so proud. He'd simply have to be more careful. And he'd keep an eye out for Jiri's battalion, wherever it might be stationed between Springfield and Rolla.

As soon as he was well away from the Rebel camp, he left the dusty road and sat in the shade of a tree. There he ate some of the meat and bread Mrs. Ray had packed for him.

When he had finished eating, Mike stretched and looked around. Not far from him, on the other side of the split-rail fence that edged a farmer's property, a young woman was climbing a path leading from a springhouse to the farmhouse and carrying a bucket of water. Sprays of crystal drops splashed over the edge of the bucket as she took a step off balance. Mike licked his lips, imagining the wonderful taste of the sweet chilled water. Just what he needed after eating salty meat on this hot day!

Leaning on the top rail, he called out, "Miss? Could you spare a cup of water?"

The girl stopped and appraised him with unsmiling eyes. He saw then that she was even younger than he first thought. "What are your sympathies—Union or Confederate?" she called back.

Mike tried a pleasant grin. "I'm just asking for a cool drink of water. What difference does it make where my sympathies lie?"

"It matters," she said. "I'd sooner pour this water into the ground than give it to anyone who supported those secessionist bullies who trampled our garden and stole our horses and food!"

With a guilty pang Mike thought of Janie, whose family's stores his own company had taken under the order to forage. "I'm sorry," he said sadly, as much to Janie as to the girl who stood before him. "I'm not a southern sympathizer, but I won't bother you again."

As he turned and limped toward the road, the girl called, "Wait!" Soon she was beside the fence, a battered tin cup of water cradled in her hands. Unsmiling, she held it out toward Mike.

The sun beat down on his head and shoulders with such force, Mike gladly took the water and gulped it down. "Thanks," he said as he handed back the cup.

"I wish I could offer you food," she said, "but the Rebs have taken everything. Last week a dozen or so broke into our house and demanded that Ma cook them supper. When she tried to explain how little food we had, they began smashing her china." Her eyes reddened as she added, "Her own mother's china. Someday it would have been mine."

"I'm sorry," Mike said. "At least the Union—"

"Union soldiers aren't any better," she said through tightened lips. "When General Lyon first came into Springfield, he sent his bodyguard ahead of him, and they did a thorough job of sacking the town."

Mike was puzzled. "But from what you said earlier, I thought you were against only the Rebs."

"My father's a Union soldier," she answered. Again tears came to her eyes. "But I know Pa would never break into a house and steal things and force the women to cook for him. He'd never do that. He's a good and gentle man."

Mike asked, "Why don't you leave Springfield? Maybe your family could go to a safer place until the war's over."

"This land is all we own," the girl said. "Besides, there's nowhere we could go."

"Don't you have other family—cousins? Aunts and uncles? Grandparents, maybe? Isn't there someone somewhere who could take you in?"

"No," the girl answered. Dangling the cup on one finger, she stepped back from the fence. "I have to get that water into the kitchen. Ma will be wondering where I am."

"Thanks again for the drink," Mike said.

The girl's eyes were dark with sorrow, but her voice was soft and gentle. "Wherever you're off to, may you have a safe journey."

"And may you and your family be safe," Mike answered. Sadly he watched her hoist the heavy bucket before he climbed down to the road and joined the traffic moving into Springfield. With luck he'd find a barn to sleep in for the night and in the morning meet up with someone who'd give him a ride to Rolla and to his company. If Jiri's battalion was still near Rolla, Mike might have a chance of finding him. And then Emily would have something of Todd's that she could always treasure.

Mike thought of how the girl with the water had lost her grandmother's china to a mean, rotten bully. He wouldn't allow the watch meant for Emily to meet the same fate.

13

Mike was surprised by what he saw in Springfield. Although some of the people who lived there seemed to be going about their business as usual, many of the tidy houses, shaded by trees and bordered by flowers, stood empty; and a number of store windows were boarded up. A smattering of wagons filled with household possessions, their passengers often only women and children, headed in one direction—north from Springfield.

As it grew dark, Mike passed a trim two-story house whose front door hung open. He walked up the steps and entered, calling loudly, but no one answered.

He closed the door and looked around. There were a few candles still in their holders, and most of the furniture was in place, but the house looked bare, as though the people who had lived in it had stripped it of photographs and family treasures and loving memories, carrying them away as they fled.

Mike walked through all the rooms, upstairs and down,

just to make sure he was alone in the house. Relaxing as he felt more secure, he closed the heavy window drapes, lit the candles, and ate more of the food Mrs. Ray had given him. When he finished eating, Mike wrapped up the remainder, knowing it would be scant fare for tomorrow's journey, and replaced it in his knapsack, which he leaned against a small table that stood under a window.

Mike reminded himself that upstairs he could have his choice of comfortable beds. He lit a candle and made his way up the stairs and into the largest bedroom, in which earlier he'd spotted a huge tester bed with a thick feather mattress. Snuffing out the candle, he threw himself into the bed facedown and sighed with pleasure.

He awoke to the sound of glass smashing against a wall, and a man's angry shout, "Somebody took away all the valuables!"

Another man belched loudly and laughed. "You've got more than you can carry already. Are you going to take 'em into battle with you?"

Soldiers? Mike tiptoed to the top of the stairs, looked down, and saw a whole group of Rebs—four? Five? And they were all very drunk.

One soldier gave a nasty chuckle and said, "Augie's found a good place to peddle what he collects. Treat him right, and maybe he'll share what he knows with you."

Another belch, another mumble—Mike couldn't make it out—before the soldier said, "All I want now is a soft bed."

A long shadow leapt up the stairs, and Mike jumped back. As quietly as he could, he raised the bedroom window in search of an escape route.

What good luck! Branches of a large tree swept against the roof of the house. Mike swung his legs over the windowsill and balanced easily on the roof as he lowered the window. As candlelight suddenly flooded the doorway of the bedroom, Mike flattened himself to the side of the casement and peered cautiously through the window. A squat, bulky man stumbled to the dresser, barely managing to place his candle on it before he fell across the bed.

Right where I was sleeping! Mike thought with a shiver.

Mike followed the nearest and sturdiest branch to the trunk of the tree and climbed halfway to the ground before a horrible thought struck him: *My knapsack! It's in the parlor!*

He reached the last branch and dropped silently to the ground, grinding his teeth as pain seared his leg. Stopping only to try to rub the pain away, Mike crept cautiously to the nearest parlor window. If he remembered correctly, his knapsack was directly under this window.

Slowly, Mike raised the sash barely an inch—just high enough to reach in with one finger. He pushed the drapes apart, creating a peephole. Mike examined the room, inch by inch, finally reassuring himself that the room was empty.

Mike shoved again at the wooden window frame. Good! The sash slid up silently and easily. Pausing only for another careful look around, Mike hoisted himself onto the windowsill and pushed the table below to one side.

As the table legs squeaked across the polished floor, Mike froze, listening, waiting, but the house remained silent. He dropped noiselessly to the floor and scooped up his knapsack with a sigh of relief, slipping his arms into the straps.

Mike grasped the window frame, ready to jump outside, when a deep voice behind him growled, "Stay where you are, and turn around!"

His heart hammering, Mike turned and saw a Confederate soldier pointing a musket in his direction. Mike shouted, "Don't shoot! The silver's hidden in the attic!"

Later, Mike thought about the expressions of surprise and greed that swept over the Reb's face, but at the moment he had time only to think of his escape. He leapt up and dove headfirst through the open window, as musket fire splintered the window frame next to his head.

Scrambling like a four-footed animal, Mike reached the protection of a high hedge that bordered the yard. No one followed him. No one even came to the window. He grinned as he thought of the rowdy drunken procession of soldiers climbing to the attic, searching and searching for something that wasn't there. Judging from the look of the house, any silver owned by the people who had fled from Springfield had gone with them.

Mike ducked through the hedge and into the yard behind the house to the next street, limping and stumbling in an uneven jog-trot until he was out of the town itself and into the rural countryside.

At most of the darkened farmhouses dogs barked a warning, and Mike plodded on; but finally he arrived at a house with a barn not too far from the road, where only silence greeted him. Ready at any sign of danger to turn tail and run or flatten himself in the tall grass, Mike cautiously climbed over the split-rail fence and walked through the pasture toward the barn.

The small barn door opened easily, and Mike—breathing in the familiar pungent odors of animal sweat, urine, and hay—felt his way along the stalls to a ladder. As horses snuffled and snorted and a few chickens sleepily scolded whoever had interrupted their sleep, Mike spoke to them soothingly and softly. He climbed to a loft and lay in the loose hay, tucking his knapsack under his head as his pillow.

It surprised him that this farm's livestock had been undisturbed. Most of the countryside where the armies had marched had been foraged. Pillaged. Plundered. Looted. There were many names for stealing someone's property, but whatever the reasons behind the thefts, Mike hated them as much as he hated unwelcome memories of his days as a copper thief.

* * *

The next morning, Mike awoke to bright sunlight. He stretched and yawned noisily before he realized there were sounds below him in the barn. Startled, he sat up, fully alert as a woman's voice called out, "Who's up there? Speak up, or I'll yell for my husband, who'll bring his gun!"

Mike's heart raced as he slipped his arms into the straps on his knapsack and rolled to the edge of the loft. Grasping the top of the ladder for support, he leaned out so the woman could see him. "It's just me, ma'am. My name's Mike Kelly. I'm traveling through and needed a bed for the night."

The woman looked like many of the other farm women Mike had seen lately: faded print dress, hair pulled back into a bun, weathered skin dried into early wrinkles, and callused hands with stubby fingernails. But this woman was gripping a pitchfork, and there was fear in her eyes.

"Come down careful-like," she said, and Mike hurried to obey.

He stood in front of her, brushing hay from his clothes and smiling in friendship, thankful when the fear left her eyes and she leaned the pitchfork against the nearest stall.

"You're only a boy," she said.

"Yes, ma'am," Mike answered.

"Where's your family?"

"Spread out," he said. "Some in and near St. Joseph, some in Kansas."

"Is that where you're off to now? St. Joseph?"

Mike was tired of trying to dodge the truth. Even with a sore leg, he knew he could outrun this woman if need be, so he told her honestly, "I was wounded in the battle at Wilson's Creek, but I'm healed enough now to join my company. I think they're up near Rolla."

Her eyes widened with surprise. "You're too young to be a soldier."

"I'm a musician," Mike said proudly. "A drummer."

She shook her head in exasperation and repeated, "Too

young. Much too young." Suddenly her eyes narrowed. "You're Confederate, aren't you?"

Mike took a deep breath. "No, ma'am," he said. "Union Army."

Fear returned to the woman's face, and she quickly glanced at the open barn doors. Dropping her voice, she said, "Get out of here quickly. My husband's got a vendetta against Union sympathizers. If he—"

The pattern of sunlight shifted as a large figure entered the doorway. "What's this, Essie? Who've you got there?"

"Just a boy, Henry," Essie answered firmly, although Mike could see her hands tremble. "Name's Mike Kelly, and he's goin' through to join family. He needed a place to sleep and picked our barn."

As Henry strode toward him, Mike felt as if he'd landed in the path of a giant locomotive. It was all he could do to keep from turning to run, but he knew this man would be too much for him.

Henry, his skin a mottled red and puffy with extra weight, loomed over Mike, taking plenty of time to study him. "He's just a boy," he finally said.

"That's what I told you," Essie mumbled.

"You got any hard cash, boy?" Henry boomed out.

Mike shook his head. "Not even a cent."

"Whatcha got in your knapsack?"

The uniform again! "Just a few clothes," Mike said. For an instant his knees wobbled, and he grabbed the ladder for support.

Essie stepped forward and put a steadying arm around Mike, who limped as she guided him toward the door. "Henry, it's plain to see Mike Kelly is hungry. And he's hurt. Look at the way he's limping. I'll feed him breakfast before we send him on his way."

Henry didn't give up. "What happened to your leg, boy?"

"I fell," Mike said.

"Cut it open, huh?" For some reason Henry chuckled.

"Well, if Essie's soft-hearted enough to want to feed you, then I won't object." He scowled at Essie. "No meat, though. The sausage we keep for ourselves."

Essie didn't answer, but once she had led Mike inside the kitchen, she began to pan-fry a couple of slices of pork sausage.

Settled into a rush-back chair at the kitchen table, Mike blurted out, "Aren't you afraid to cook the sausage? Won't it make him angry?"

Essie gripped the spatula, and her lips became stretched and tight before she answered. "Henry's my husband, and for the most part I've always done what he said because I had no cause not to. But I can't go along with the way he's hurting neighbors and former friends who are Union sympathizers—reporting them to the Confederates, riding with those military bushwackers to burn their barns and houses . . . stealing, hating—" Her voice broke. She turned away, cracking two eggs and dropping the contents into the sausage grease.

"Does your husband own slaves?" Mike asked.

Essie turned and looked at him, indignation on her face. "Not a one!" she said. "And neither do a lot of the folks who are against the Union. They stand on the principle that government shouldn't have a say-so in people's private lives.

"To my way of thinking, the slavery issue is just an excuse to allow some people to do hateful things and feel righteous about it. I know that's all it is for Henry." A tear ran down her cheek. "It's turned some of our friends against us. It's turned me against my own husband."

Mike didn't know what to say. He wanted to cheer the kind woman up, so he said, "Maybe the war will be over soon, and things will get better."

"Things will never get better," Essie said in a dull, tired voice. She reached for a plate on which she'd sliced some bread and added the sausage and eggs.

Mike didn't try to make conversation. He ate ravenously.

After washing up at the pump outside, he thanked Essie again and limped back to the road to Rolla, where he was lucky enough to pick up a ride with a farmer who was going as far as Lebanon. Mike finished the food Mrs. Ray had packed for him and spent the night sleeping under a tree.

For the next two days he walked, sometimes riding short distances, and gradually he came closer to Rolla. Although he was headed for his company and anxious to learn the fate of some of his friends, he couldn't get Jiri's evil grin out of his mind. So along the way, if the opportunity presented itself, he asked passersby, "Is there a Confederate encampment nearby?"

A few people assured him that last they'd heard, a small group of Confederate cavalry on an exploratory mission was up ahead, camped in a clearing some twenty miles or so east of Rolla.

"Stay on this road and you can't miss 'em," an elderly man told Mike. He winked. "Gonna join up?"

"I'm too young," Mike said, and stepped back into the road, wanting to get away from the man and his questions.

But the man shouted after him, "If'n I was young and healthy, I'd be off to join up, too. Got to beat those Yankees who come down here tryin' to tell us what to do."

Mike knew better than to answer the way he'd like to. He just plodded along the road, hoping to pick up a ride with another wagon driver.

As he drew closer and closer to Rolla, a spark tingled through Mike's body. With any luck, he'd soon catch up to Jiri. And no matter how brutal and ruthless Jiri was, Mike would have to outwit him. He was determined to get Todd's pocket watch and take it back to Emily Blakely. He'd promised.

14

IN THIS HILLY, forested countryside, Mike found few farms, but late that night he came upon a roadside tavern with a half-dozen horses tethered outside. Mike's nose, quivering at the fragrance of roasted meat, led him straight through the smoky, noisy room to the tavern keeper.

"I'll clean up for you," Mike said, "if you'll give me something to eat."

The man wiped his hands on a dirty apron tied around his bulging middle and stared sternly down at Mike. "Folks who come here pay for their food and drink."

"My pockets are as empty as my belly," Mike said.

The tavern keeper laughed. "Very well, a fair exchange. Roast chicken and bread in exchange for a clean kitchen." He paused and said kindly, "And if you want to sleep in front of the fireplace tonight, I'll have no objections."

"Thanks," Mike said. He held out his right hand. "The name's Mike Kelly."

"Knew you were Irish when I spotted that red hair." The

tavern keeper shook Mike's hand and smiled. "Around these parts I'm known as Pat Duffy." With his chin he nodded in the direction of a back room. "There's a cupboard just inside the kitchen where you can put your belongings. Rest easy. They'll be safe enough."

Mike found the cupboard easily and stashed his knapsack in it. When he returned to the counter, Mr. Duffy handed him a heaping plate of food, which Mike took to a table off in a corner. Delicious! He stuffed himself with roasted chicken, thinking of nothing beyond his plate, until a conversation at the next table caught his attention. "Think those Confederates will be in here tonight?"

"I hope not. That one—the blond sneaky kind of feller—I wouldn't say it to his face, but I suspect he cheats at cards."

Mike nearly dropped the chicken leg he was holding. *Jiri!* That meant his unit hadn't left their encampment in the area! And Jiri was still up to his tricks of cheating people. Mike couldn't believe it. The biggest hoodlum in the entire Confederacy had stolen Todd's watch! Mike's mind raced. *If Jiri's coming here, I'll have to stay out of sight. Will Jiri have Todd's watch on him? And if he does . . . ?*

One of the men put an abrupt stop to Mike's panic when he told his friends, "There's no chance you'll see 'em tonight —or any other night in the near future. Their party was fixin' to leave today and head north."

"North to where?" someone asked. "Are we lookin' at another battle?"

"Not unless they're goin' to rendezvous with the whole of Price's army and then some. I heard they were off toward Jefferson City."

"Then they may meet up with Frémont. Think they can take him single-handedly?"

There was general laughter, and the conversation shifted to local gossip.

How was he ever going to catch up with Jiri Logan and retrieve Todd's watch? He'd come so close and had missed

Jiri by only a day! Frustrated, Mike wiped his greasy hands on his pants legs and climbed off the stool, carrying his plate to a back room where other dirty dishes were stacked.

Mike had made a bargain, and he intended to keep it. He stirred up the smoldering fire in the fireplace, filled the kettle with water from a pump near the back door, and hung it on a hook over the fire. He emptied the sink, wiped it free of food and grease, and found a small sharp knife to cut slivers from a large chunk of lye soap.

When the water was hot enough to melt the soap, Mike plunged his hands into the suds and scrubbed the plates and cups in the dishpan with all his energy, getting rid of some of the anger and frustration he felt about Jiri.

When Mike reentered the main room of the tavern, he froze. In the center of the room, at a table with two other Rebel soldiers and some of the local men, sat Jiri.

Jiri's eyes were on the cards he was dealing, and the other players watched just as intently, so none of them noticed Mike.

Mike turned and slipped out of the room. Leaning against the wall for support and breathing deeply, willing his heart to stop banging against his chest, Mike tried to think clearly.

It seemed logical that the Confederate detail hadn't left the neighborhood yet, but they were bound to be packed and ready. Jiri would probably have Todd's watch either on his person or in his saddlebags.

The saddlebags would be an easy place to begin his search. Mike slipped out the back door. Circling the building, he discovered three horses carrying Confederate Army saddles, pouches, and bedrolls. The horses were tethered with other horses to the rail that ran across the front of the tavern. The Rebel cavalry must be planning to get under way at first light, and these three Rebs—packed and ready to go—had probably decided to spend their last night in the area at the tavern.

There was no way Mike could tell which of the Confederate horses belonged to Jiri. He might have to go through all the saddlebags. He spoke quietly to the first horse, a spotted gray, and stroked his neck until the animal stopped its nervous stomping and whinnying. Then Mike opened the clasp nearest to him and reached inside. He pulled out a fistful of papers—among them a girl's photograph and a letter addressed to Sergeant Tom McKinney.

As fast as he could, Mike shoved the papers back and moved to the next horse, a tan with white markings on his legs and forehead. The horse seemed to sense Mike's nervousness and shied away from him, bobbing its head, snorting, and stamping.

Mike finally managed to soothe the horse, but the commotion had made the other horses nervous and noisy. What if Mike was discovered? With shaking fingers he unfastened the clasp on the saddlebag, reached inside, and gasped as his fingers touched something round and cold. The watch!

As Mike tried to grasp the watch, it slid from his fingers, dropping to the bottom of the pouch. Mike stood on tiptoe, shoving his hand more deeply into the pouch. But the horse backed sideways, away from him, and he stumbled, nearly falling under the animal's feet. As the first horse whinnied and the third horse snorted and stamped, Mike clung to the saddle, trying to regain his footing.

Suddenly the tavern door opened and someone yelled, "Who's out there with the horses? What are you up to?"

"It's the army horses that are actin' up," a man said.

Then Mike heard a familiar voice that sent chills up his backbone. "Whoever's out there won't cause trouble for long."

Jiri!

"Now, wait!" Mr. Duffy bellowed. "There's no call to shoot anyone. Put the handgun away."

"You there!" Jiri called out, ignoring Mr. Duffy. "Move

away from those horses! Put your hands up and come out slowly."

Mike had no intention of facing Jiri. He knew that the underbrush was thick along the side of the road, the forest deep and dark. He picked up a small stone and skittered it along the dirt under the horses' feet. As the startled animals snorted and stomped, Mike bent low and dashed silently down the road and into the forest.

Well away from the tavern, Mike settled down under a tree and tried unsuccessfully to sleep. His heart still raced, and his mind churned with anger both at Jiri and at himself for so narrowly missing his opportunity. He had touched the watch. He was sure of it. He had actually come that close to the watch, dropped it, and lost his only chance!

"Oh, Da," Mike whispered aloud. "How am I going to keep my promise to Todd? What should I do?"

First things first, the answer came. For a moment Mike didn't know what the words meant, until he remembered his promise to Pat Duffy. *In the morning, when his customers have left, I'll fulfill my part of the bargain*, Mike thought. *And come to think of it, I'll have to return anyway to collect my knapsack.* More at peace with himself, Mike curled up and fell asleep.

It was still dark when Mike awoke and made his way back to the tavern. The horses were gone and the building was dark and silent, but Mike approached cautiously.

He'd already determined that there was no room for living quarters in the tavern, so he'd have the place to himself. He tried the front door, only to find it padlocked. He checked the back door next, but it too was locked. Mike was undaunted. There must be a window to open. Sure enough, he soon found one next to the back stoop. Mike slid it open and climbed inside the kitchen.

The fire in the fireplace still glowed, so it was easy to add kindling and wood and bring it to life again. Then Mike set about completing his chores. With cloths and hot soapy water Mike tackled the greasy tables and chairs, then swept the floor. Pleased with his work, he attacked the remaining dirty dishes, put them up on the shelves, and poured the wash water out the back door.

The sky slowly softened to gray, and Mike knew it was time to be on his way. "I did a good job, Da," he whispered. "You can be proud of me."

All was in order and the fire low again, in no need of banking, so Mike opened the cupboard and reached for his knapsack.

To his surprise, an envelope lay on top of his knapsack. He opened it and found a few bills and a note from Mr. Duffy: *Knew you'd be back. Have a safe journey.*

Gratefully, Mike tucked the note and the money into his knapsack. The cash would serve him well.

He left the tavern through the window and pulled the sash back into place. By nightfall, he should reach Rolla and rejoin his company. With a new drum and drumsticks, he'd soon be ready to take his place in battle again, and maybe he'd meet up once more with Jiri Logan.

Mike had trudged for only a short while when a wagon driver stopped and offered him a lift. "Goin' into Rolla?" the man asked, and when Mike nodded eagerly, he offered, "Climb in the back. There's room between the potato sacks."

In a way Mike was glad to be relegated to the wagon bed. The potato sacks made a lumpy but not too uncomfortable cushion—and a good hiding place in the event they met up with a Confederate patrol.

There was no sign of Rebel cavalry, however. Mike deduced that the soldiers had abandoned their camp and followed a side road north to Jefferson City. He lay back to relax, staring up at the bright blue sky, glad that soon he would return to his company.

* * *

After hours of light sleep and anticipation, Mike at last stood by the Union Army camp outside the town of Rolla.

But instead of bounding toward the encampment, as he'd expected to do, Mike felt such a heavy mixture of pride and dread that he was unable to move from the roadway. He watched the activity at the gate as though he were a stranger and not a loyal drummer returning to duty. This was his company, where he belonged, yet his captain had been killed. . . . Ben, the Kansas volunteer so eager to return home when his three-month tour of duty was up, had been shot dead as well. And Todd was doubly violated—killed and robbed of the one thing he valued most.

The same fearful visions Mike had tried to forget—splattered blood, screaming wounded, and the pounding roar of the fight at Wilson's Creek—rushed back into his mind with renewed force. As frantically as he tried, he was powerless to push them away. War, no matter its purpose, was a horrendous nightmare made real. Mike remembered when he and Todd had thought that joining the army would be a great, exciting adventure. He couldn't believe he'd been so wrong.

But for all the brutality of battle, he had signed on to help put an end to slavery by serving his country, and now it was time to report for duty. Mike limped to the guard at the gate.

Before he could identify himself, someone shouted, "Mike Kelly! It's really you! We all thought sure you were a goner!"

"Billy Whitley!" Mike exclaimed with enormous relief as he looked up to see the familiar face. But the relief was short-lived as Mike remembered that he didn't know to whom he should report. He said to the guard, "My captain was Captain Dawes of the Second Kansas Infantry, killed at Wilson's Creek."

"We'll find Sergeant Gridley," Billy offered. "He'll fix things right for you."

"How about Harley?" Mike asked quietly.

"Harley's here," Billy answered, and Mike let out a long breath of relief.

As they walked through the camp, Billy chuckled. "Thought we'd be home by now, didn't we? Those Rebs really fooled us."

"Have you heard where we'll go next?" Mike asked, raising his voice over the bustle going on around him.

"Harley says he heard that General Frémont plans to march down from Jefferson City and retake Springfield."

Mike thought sorrowfully about the people who had remained in and near the battered town of Springfield. How were they going to withstand another attack?

Billy raised one hand and let out a "halloo!" and Mike looked up to see Sergeant Gridley. As fast as he could, Mike limped toward his sergeant and shouted, "Michael Kelly reporting for duty, sir!"

Sergeant Gridley stopped abruptly as he watched Mike approach. "Mr. Kelly," he said, returning Mike's salute, "you weren't listed among our wounded. We feared you were dead."

"I was badly hurt, sir," Mike explained in a rush of words. "The Confederate surgeon wanted to take my leg, but the lady of that farmhouse that was in the thick of the battle took me in. She cleaned the wound and tended me until I could walk again." Mike puffed out his chest. "And now I'm as fit as ever."

The sergeant squatted and shoved up the right leg of Mike's trousers, whistling as he saw the size of the scar. He touched the leg, and Mike winced. "Still hurts a lot, doesn't it?" Sergeant Gridley asked.

"Hardly at all," Mike blustered. "My leg grows stronger every day."

Sergeant Gridley stood and slowly shook his head. "Mike, you wouldn't be able to keep up with us on a march, and I'm guessing it'll be this way for quite some time. That's a bad wound. I'm going to fill out the papers needed to give you an honorable discharge."

Dismayed, Mike stammered, "B-but the company needs me!"

"It needs men who are fit to stand the rigors of a march into battle. Go home, Mr. Kelly, and get well again. Grow a couple of years older and a couple of inches taller. Then we'll be glad to see you reenlist."

As the drum call to supper rolled through camp, Mike's fingers instinctively reached for invisible drumsticks. Heartsick at the thought that his drum was truly lost forever and his days as an army musician brought to an end, Mike stared at the ground, unable to look at the man who was so easily dismissing him.

But Sergeant Gridley clapped a hand on Mike's shoulder. "There's been much talk around camp about how brave you were, how you stood your post no matter how thick the fighting around you. Captain Dawes was proud of you. I am, too. And I see no reason why there won't be a letter of commendation for you."

The words he wanted to say stuck in Mike's throat, but Sergeant Gridley didn't seem to notice his anguish. "Now come with me, Mr. Kelly. I think a large plate of stew is just what you need."

Supper with his company did, in fact, prove healing. Harley greeted Mike with a warm bear hug, and some of the other men gathered around, too. The evening was filled with reminiscences of some of the humorous stories that had been told, the practical jokes that had been played, and all that had gone on since the Battle of Wilson's Creek. The terrible hurt that had filled Mike's entire body and mind began to dissipate, and Mike told the men of his journey from Wilson's Creek.

There were sly nudges when he described the girl who gave him water, whoops when he told about nearly getting captured in the house in Springfield, mutterings when he related the story of the farmer who rode in secret to burn the homes and barns of Union sympathizers, and angry grumbling as he told about Jiri's theft of Todd's watch.

"But tomorrow I'll be on my way home to Fort Leavenworth," Mike said bitterly. "Because of my leg wound, I've been discharged from the army."

"That's the way it has to be," Harley said. "Anyone experienced in battle knows that every member of a company depends on the others. One weak link breaks a chain."

"I thought you didn't have a home," one of the men said. "Heard you was an orphan."

Embarrassed, Mike shrugged. "Captain Dawes decided I must be an orphan after I told him I came west on one of the orphan trains, and I let him think so because I wanted so much to be an army drummer. But I'm not really an orphan. Ma gave me up to the Children's Aid Society, along with my sisters and brothers, to be placed in foster homes because" —Mike gulped and left out the part about his arrest for copper stealing—"because she couldn't take care of us in New York City."

"How does Fort Leavenworth come into it?"

"Captain Joshua Taylor and his wife took me in. The captain's with his company in Virginia, and Louisa, my foster mother . . ." Mike sighed. "I had to do something—anything—to help, so I ran away. That is, Todd and I ran away together—to join the Union Army."

After telling his secrets, Mike expected disapproval, but the men nodded as though Mike's decisions were strictly his own business.

"Which way will you travel to reach home?" Billy asked. "You'd better not go back through Springfield."

"He'll go by way of the river," Harley said. "It's the best choice. There may be a few mounted Confederate details scattered throughout the countryside, but General Frémont's gathering his army in Jefferson City, and Mike will be safer taking that route than any other. Jefferson City's right on the Missouri River, and there'll be paddlewheelers headed for St. Joe to carry our lad as far as Kansas City or Fort Leavenworth."

"St. Joe," Mike murmured in a sudden burst of homesickness. "Maybe I'll travel to St. Joe and visit my mother before going back to the fort. That's where Ma lives now." But suddenly, the rest of what Harley had said hit him with such a punch he gasped for breath: *Jefferson City! Where Jiri Logan was headed!* If Jiri were anywhere in the vicinity of Jefferson City, Mike would find him.

15

AFTER SUPPER SERGEANT Gridley handed Mike a pair of wool and rubber blankets and a thick packet of envelopes. "Mail from your family," he said with a smile. "Since we were waiting for further word about your whereabouts, I didn't return these with letters of condolence. So as far as your family's concerned, you've remained safe and sound."

As Mike clutched the letters eagerly, the sergeant added, "I've assigned you to Harley's tent. Get a good night's sleep and a good breakfast in the morning, and we'll send you off with as much food as we can spare and this bedroll as our parting gift."

Mike spread out the blankets and sat upon them cross-legged, happily reading his mail. Ma had written four letters, each of which included notes from Peg; Louisa, Frances, and Megan had written three times, but Danny had written just once. There was even a letter from Captain—now Major Taylor, and Mike tore the envelope open with trembling fingers. What if the major were displeased with him?

After reading just a few words Mike settled down comfortably. Major Taylor had written his feelings the way any father would have. "I understand your eagerness to serve the Union, and I'm proud of you for it," the major wrote. "However, you're but a boy, and I'm greatly concerned for your safety. When your ninety-day contract is up, I want you to return to Fort Leavenworth."

There was advice—lots of it—but a strong, fatherly love came through in every word.

Mike yearned for the war to end and for Major Taylor to return to Fort Leavenworth. More than anything, Mike wanted a father close at hand.

The remaining letters were both warm and worried in tone. Each shared small funny family doings, as well as concerns about local problems or the actions of southern sympathizers. Danny's foster parents had been taunted repeatedly by a neighbor who resented their stand for the Union, and Danny complained bitterly about being too young to join the Union Army.

"Whatever you do, Mike, that's what I want to do, too," Danny wrote, bragging, "I've been practicing with Alfrid's rifle, and you'd be surprised what a good shot I am."

But Mike was far from sorry that Danny wasn't using that rifle in battle. It was with a great sense of relief that Mike visualized his once tag-along younger brother safely at home, with Alfrid and Ennie Swenson to care for him. With any luck the war would be over soon, and Danny would never see the horrors that Mike had seen or be surrounded by terrors like those Mike could never forget.

Mike had no sooner finished reading the letters than Billy Whitley settled down next to him. Billy held out some paper, envelopes, and a pencil. "In case you don't have any writin' materials left, I'm glad to share mine."

"I can pay you," Mike offered, thinking of the money in his pocket, but Billy shook his head.

"No need to. In return, you can do me a favor."

"Glad to," Mike said easily. "What is it?"

Billy pulled out a thin gold pocket watch with a delicately etched design on its lid, and held it up, dangling on its chain. "I've been thinkin' about Todd's watch and what's come of it, instead of his sister gettin' it, the way Todd wanted. This was my pa's watch, and there's no reason for me to be takin' it into battle and maybe losin' it or maybe a bullet ruinin' it, when by all rights my wife Aggie should have it." He looked at Mike pleadingly. "Will you take it to Aggie for me? She's gone with the children to stay with relations in St. Joe. If you're goin' through St. Joe, you could deliver this easy."

Mike nodded. "Write down your wife's name and where I can find her, and I'll get the watch to her."

"Thanks!" Billy clapped a hand on Mike's shoulder, and immediately set about writing the address, along with a note to Aggie. He put the papers with the watch inside an envelope.

Mike tucked the envelope into his pocket and began to answer his letters. As he wrote, Mike thought about the sad eyes of the girl who had given him a drink of water and the frightened eyes of the housewife who had begun to hate her husband. There was so much to write about, so much to tell, but Mike wrote only that he had rejoined his company and would soon be discharged and sent home.

In his letter to his mother he added that he'd stop off in St. Joe for a few days to visit. In his letter to Danny he wrote that while he was in St. Joe he'd make a trip to the Swensons' farm so the two of them could be together again, even if just for a little while.

In the morning, after breakfast, Mike left camp with his papers and provisions and caught a ride with a sutler traveling to Jefferson City.

The hilly countryside, with its splotches of sunlit meadows and shade-cool forests, was beautiful, and the sutler confided to Mike that he was glad to have company on the long trip.

"If we meet up with any Confederate patrols, I've got a near-empty wagon and a small amount of cash in my pocket." He winked and added, "Just enough to satisfy 'em so they'll take it and let us go on our way."

To Mike's relief, they did not meet up with Confederate soldiers, and at the end of the second day they arrived without mishap in "Jeff City," as the sutler called it. Even though the town was the capital of Missouri and probably bustling with business during daylight hours, at this time of late evening not too many people were out on the streets. Mike stopped a shopkeeper who was locking his doors, to ask if Jefferson City was still under General Frémont's control, only to discover that Frémont's army had left camp and had begun its trek south to Springfield.

"Now, if it's Confederate soldiers you're lookin' for, you're in better luck," the shopkeeper told Mike with a wink and a teasing grin. "A couple of patrols are in the area, and they've been showin' up here from time to time."

Mike spoke up boldly, his mind on Jiri. "Where will I find these Confederates?"

The shopkeeper looked at Mike in surprise. "If I were you, I wouldn't try too hard to find them," he said. "They're much more likely to find *you*."

But Mike searched for Rebels nonetheless, walking the streets where taverns were to be found, looking in vain for horses with Confederate Army trappings.

His wanderings took him down to the landing where, among countless riverboats, a large sternwheeler was moored, its white paint gleaming brightly in the light from the dockside oil lamps. Mike leaned against a shuttered storefront in the shadows, awed by the ornate three-story floating giant.

Suddenly, a slender figure appeared on the empty deck of the nearest boat and ran down a narrow gangplank to the dock, pausing under one of the hanging oil lamps. "Jim!" Mike whispered as he recognized his old friend who had traveled west with him on an orphan train. He hurried forward, calling, "Jim? Jim Riley?"

"Mike!" Jim shouted as Mike came into the pool of light. "I never thought I'd see you here!"

Since their last meeting, Jim had grown taller and more muscular, and the sun had browned his skin. Mike clapped Jim's shoulder. Grinning, Jim poked Mike's arm with his fist. "I guess you got what you wanted," Mike said, glancing at the docked paddlewheeler. "You told us you'd get adopted by a family who lived by the river."

"It didn't work out exactly that way," Jim answered, and Mike caught a flash of sorrow in his eyes. "I ran away, drifted down here, and found work as a deckhand on the *Mary Belle.*" Jim put an arm around Mike's shoulders and guided him to a bench under one of the lamps. "You're limping," he said. "What happened to you?"

Mike flopped onto the bench next to Jim and told him briefly what had taken place in his life since they'd parted in St. Joe.

"Shot in the leg in battle?" Jim slowly shook his head in wonder. "Mike Kelly a drummer in the Union Army? Never would the boys back on the New York docks believe a wild tale like that!"

They laughed, but Mike soon turned serious. "I'm being sent home to heal. I need to find out if there's a steamboat headed upriver to St. Joe."

Jim jumped to his feet. "The *Mary Belle* is! One of the few passenger boats left after the army commandeered most of them. And yours truly"—he thumped his chest—"is traveling with the *Mary Belle*, polishing brass, oiling machinery, scrubbing decks, and slaving at whatever else the second mate can find to keep me busy twenty-four hours day and night."

Mike got to his feet, balancing his knapsack and bedroll. "Can I get a ticket this time of evening?"

"No, but you've got plenty of time," Jim told him. "The *Mary Belle* isn't due to shove off until ten o'clock tomorrow morning." He paused and studied Mike. "Have you got the price of a ticket?"

"Depends," Mike said. "What's the cost?"

"A cabin and three meals a day all the way to St. Joe will set you back forty to fifty dollars."

Mike whistled. "I haven't got near enough."

"Never mind," Jim said. "Seven dollars will buy you a place to sleep outside on one of the decks. Since you've got a bedroll, that shouldn't be a problem, and you can bring along your own food."

When Mike didn't answer, Jim said, "You haven't got seven dollars either?"

"Closer to five," Mike told him, "and some of that I'd need to use to buy food for the trip."

"Come on," Jim said cheerfully, and led the way toward the darkened boat. "You can sleep in my cabin tonight, and if Seth, the second mate, is in the same tavern he usually frequents, we'll find him and remind him that he can use another deckhand, now that Oliver's quit."

Jim led Mike on a tour through the boat, showing him everything from some of the fancy cabins, with their chandeliers and puffy coverlets on the beds, down to the boiler room, which was much more familiar to Jim. Finally, Mike and Jim settled into a cabin with space for little more than the two bunks that nearly filled it.

As they chewed hard on the tough dried beef and bread from Mike's knapsack, Mike told Jim about his friend Todd and about Jiri's theft.

Full of sympathy for his friend, Jim said, "We'll find Seth and make sure of that job for you." He stashed Mike's knapsack under his bunk behind his own possessions, then led the way to a tavern near the waterfront.

The boys found Seth at an opportune moment. He was sitting in a tavern, complaining to his friends about the shortage of good help, with so many able-bodied hands off to fight the war on either side. Mike had only to assure him that he was fit and hearty enough to work as a deckhand, and all was settled. He'd report to work early the next morning.

Once outside the tavern, Mike said, "If Jiri Logan's in Jefferson City, then he'll probably be with his friends, gambling at one of the taverns. Do you have any idea which ones the Confederates go to?"

"I might," Jim said. They followed the nearest street down two blocks to a large, brightly lit tavern. Flickering lamps reflected in the water, which seemed to leap and jump with flashes of light, but Mike's attention was drawn to the Confederate Army horses. He stopped Jim by gripping his arm.

"There's Jiri's horse!" he whispered. "Tan with white markings. I'd recognize it anywhere."

Jim looked up and down the empty street before answering, "No one's in sight. Do you want to look in the saddlebags?"

Mike smiled, even though his pulse was racing. "If I find the watch and take it, Jiri might not notice it was missing for days. He might think he lost it."

"I wouldn't be too sure," Jim said. "You tried for the watch once, and if it comes up missing, first thing off he'll suspect you were the one who lifted it."

"That may be," Mike said, "but he won't know where to find me."

Mike carefully scanned the silent street and slid quickly between the horses. "Keep watch," he whispered to Jim.

Although the horse blew through its nose and nervously high-stepped back, pulling against its tether, Mike murmured soft soothing sounds and firmly stroked the animal's neck until it relaxed.

Still speaking low to the horse, Mike gradually eased his right hand toward the saddlebag and opened the clasp. Standing on tiptoe, he reached down into the bottom of the pouch. With nervous fingers he explored inside until he touched the round cold metal of Todd's watch.

This time Mike didn't hesitate. He grasped the watch firmly and pulled it out of the saddlebag. There was enough light to examine it thoroughly, and Mike was positive it was Todd's watch. There were the tooth marks left by Todd's baby sister. This was definitely Todd's watch!

Mike fastened the clasp on the pouch again and slipped the watch into a pocket in his trousers. He stepped behind the horses and rejoined Jim, who seemed to be more interested in what Mike was doing than in watching the street.

"I've got the watch!" Mike whispered. "Let's go!"

Jim heaved a long sigh of relief. "No one's in sight," he said, and took off at a run. "Come on! Back to the boat!"

Exhilarated by his triumph, Mike couldn't resist a last glance back at the tavern. But he was unprepared for the sight of a dark shape slipping from the shadows into the lamplight. The man looked directly at Mike, then turned and entered the tavern.

16

"MIKE, WHAT'S THE matter? You look awful!" Jim said, his smile vanishing as Mike scrambled to join him at the gang-plank.

Clutching his chest as he swallowed great gulps of air, Mike managed to say, "A man was watching. I saw him. He looked right at me, then went into the tavern."

"Are you sure?" Jim asked. "I kept a sharp eye out. I didn't see anyone."

"He was standing in the shadows. I spotted him when he stepped into the light." In his fright, Mike clasped Jim's arm. "He'll tell the soldiers. I know he will."

"Why didn't he shout at us? Why'd he just watch?"

"Maybe he recognized you, Jim. If he did, he knows we'd come back to the boat."

Jim looked back along the empty landing. "If the man who saw us informed the Rebs, they'd have come after us, wouldn't they?"

Maybe Jim was right, but Mike couldn't count on it. If Jiri

knew where to find Mike, he'd be in no rush to catch him. "Is there a place I can hide on board the boat?" he asked.

Jim frowned. "Not if the Rebs make a thorough search."

Mike hobbled off the gangplank, his right leg still aching with pain. "Then I'd better find another place to sleep. Maybe there's an alley . . ."

"Not an alley!" Jim brightened and jumped down to join Mike. "I know just the spot, and I can get a key to let us in." He pointed to a narrow street that led away from the landing. "You head for the storage rooms. Fourth building down. I'll meet you there."

While Jim ran up the gangplank and disappeared into the boat, Mike hurried to the protective darkness of the street.

He had no sooner left the landing than he heard footsteps. Flattening himself against the side of the building, Mike had a clear view of men striding across the landing and up the gangplank of the *Mary Belle*. There were two in civilian clothes and three Confederate soldiers—and one of them was Jiri!

In the silence Jiri's voice carried clearly. "A boy with red hair? And you're sure he's on this boat, Mr. Groot?"

Mike's head throbbed. He took a step forward, instinctively wanting to rush to the boat to help his friend. But he stopped himself. Jim would probably have a better chance on his own. After all, Jim had a job on the boat, a right to be there.

Mike waited and watched as lanterns suddenly glowed on board the main deck. He could see the search parties moving from deck to deck, from prow to stern.

Suddenly a quick figure appeared, racing down the gangplank. "Jim!" Mike hissed as Jim entered the dark street. "Over here!"

"They didn't see me," Jim said. "Come on! Hurry! We've got to get you hidden in the storage rooms!"

Mike's leg throbbed as he ran to catch up with Jim. Finally, he reached the door that Jim held open and slipped inside.

"Where to now?" Mike asked, recovering his breath once Jim had closed and locked the door. "It's so dark in here, I can't see a thing."

Jim took Mike's arm. "Just come along with me. I know my way well. There's a path next to these boxes. It makes a turn—ooof!" Jim staggered back. "It makes a turn right here."

As they felt their way along the open path, Mike's eyes began to adjust to the darkness, and he could see boxes of all shapes and sizes.

"Some of this is cargo. It'll be carried on board in the morning," Jim told Mike. "Seth will be sure to give us the heaviest loads."

"How am I going to get on the boat?" Mike asked. "Jiri will be there looking for me."

"No, he won't," Jim said. "When he finds you're not on board, he'll leave and look elsewhere."

Jim stopped and began shoving some boxes aside. "There's a door back here," Jim said. "It leads into a room too small to bother with. That's where you're going to hide."

Jim pushed open a small door, which led to a black pit. "It's not much bigger than a cupboard," Jim said, "but at least there's enough room to lie down, so you can get some sleep tonight. I'll come back for you early in the morning, when it's time to get to work."

Mike hesitated before he entered the room. Sweat rolled down his back, and his hands were clammy. "It's like a tomb in here," he murmured.

"It's the safest place I can think of for you to hide," Jim told him. "If you like, I'll leave the door open just a crack."

"I'd like," Mike said. "Thanks."

The boxes scraped on the ground and smacked the door as Jim secured Mike into his hiding place. Mike gulped down his anxiety.

"Are you going to be all right?" Jim asked, his voice muffled through the wall of boxes.

"Sure," Mike answered bravely. Was that the scrabbling of rats in the corner? Or was his imagination playing tricks on him?

"Jim?" Mike asked, but Jim didn't answer. Mike was alone.

Mike made himself sit down and lean against the nearest wall. He could rest this way. He could even sleep.

But sleep gave him little comfort, as flashing lights and the tread of footsteps filled his dream. Worst of all, Jiri held up Todd's watch and laughed wickedly.

Waking with a start and a cry, Mike saw that the flashes of light were real, not part of a dream. He heard someone say, "Listen. Did you hear that? What was it?"

"I didn't hear anything," a man answered.

Another man laughed. "Probably a rat. You're going to find plenty of rats in these buildings near the water."

Mike would have recognized that scornful voice and laugh anywhere—Jiri's.

As quietly as he could, Mike stood and put one eye to the crack in the door. The two men stood a fair distance away, their backs to Mike's hiding place.

Carefully, Mike pulled the door completely shut and leaned against the wall, weak with fear. What if he were discovered? The men with Jiri would never believe that it was Jiri, not Mike, who had really stolen the watch. With Jiri out to get him, Mike knew he wouldn't stand a chance.

The lanterns came near, outlining the edges of the door in thin streaks of light. Close to panic, afraid to breathe, Mike tensed, waiting for the door to burst open and Jiri to appear.

But instead the light faded as the searchers moved on.

In a short while darkness closed in like a smothering blanket, and the storage rooms fell silent.

Mike's knees buckled. He slid down the wall, collapsing

onto the floor. They had gone! They hadn't found him! Exhausted from tension and sudden relief, Mike gradually fell into a deep sleep.

"Mike!" A voice interrupted his sleep. "Wake up, Mike!"

He opened his eyes to see Jim, lantern held high, peering through the open door.

"Jiri was here!" Mike mumbled.

"I know. I saw Jiri and his friends, along with Doyle—one of the ship's crew—heading for the storage rooms. I waited until they left."

"What about Doyle?" Mike asked as he crawled out of the hiding place and stretched, rubbing his stiff and aching arms and legs. "Won't Jiri have him looking for me?"

Jim shook his head. "Doyle's Federal and has no use for Jiri and his like. He'll go through the motions, but he won't help Jiri."

"Jim!" came a call from the front of the storage rooms.

"It's time to get to work," Jim said. "We've got to help load the cargo."

"Do you think I could find a cap anywhere around here?" Mike rubbed his head and tried a smile. "I'm not as sure as you are that Jiri won't still be looking for this red hair of mine."

"I thought the same," Jim said, and pulled a small-billed cap from his pocket.

"Jim? Mike? Where are you?" Seth shouted.

Jim made a face. "Back here!" he called. "We'll be right there!"

The heavy grunt work of loading and storing the cargo was only the beginning. As the sun broke the early gray of the sky, Mike found himself carrying wood to the firemen in the boiler room, polishing the brass on the inside stairways, and giving a final mop to the smudged footprints on the decks of the *Mary Belle*.

A half hour before the ten o'clock departure, Mike

headed for the top deck, carrying a rag and a tin of abrasive with which to scrub the brass fittings. But when he stepped close to the railing, he saw Jiri coming up the gangplank.

Mike stumbled back, out of Jiri's line of vision, and raced down the stairs, nearly colliding with strolling passengers who were headed for their cabins or the chairs they had bought on deck.

Stopping to regain his breath and rest his leg once he'd reached the main deck, Mike glanced into the ornate carpeted room where many passengers had gathered and saw Jiri ascending a gilded stairway that curved up to the lounge on the deck above. Good! He'd probably already been below! Trying not to attract attention, Mike ducked down the stairway to the lower deck and into Jim's cabin. Nothing seemed disturbed, and Mike's knapsack was still under Jim's bunk. Mike squirmed under the bunk and nestled behind the knapsack and Jim's store of possessions, hoping that Jiri wouldn't look there a second time.

The engines started up with such a roar, the entire boat vibrated. Mike heard the boat's huge pistons set up a regular and steady rhythm, then the slap and splash of the paddlewheel as it began to turn. As the *Mary Belle* slowly moved away from the landing, Mike was disappointed that he couldn't be on deck to see the action.

The door to Jim's cabin burst open. "Mike? Are you here?" Jim called.

"I'm under the bunk," Mike answered, and squiggled out of his hiding place. "Jiri's on the ship!" he said.

"Not now, he isn't," Jim answered. "Only passengers. Everybody else had to go ashore." He tugged at Mike's arm. "Hurry up on deck. We've got lots of work left to do, and if we're not hard at it, Seth's going to be angry."

Mike grinned. He was free of Jiri, and he could be on deck for departure. He tucked both watches into the bottom of his knapsack and reported to Seth. Before he knew it, he was coiling heavy twists of rope on the main deck starboard.

Mike had the river side of the ship almost to himself, as most of the passengers crowded to the port side, waving at friends on shore or watching the boat slip slowly past familiar landmarks. Enjoying his peaceful solitary work, Mike didn't realize anyone was approaching until a pair of boots stopped right before his face.

Mike looked up to see Jiri Logan's scowl. He jumped to his feet in terror. "W-what are you doing here?" he stammered. "Only passengers are supposed to be on board."

"So it *is* you—Corey Blair's friend," Jiri said, smug with satisfaction. "I knew you had to be the thief who stole my watch."

"The watch isn't yours, and I didn't steal it," Mike snapped. "*You* stole it! After you killed Todd."

Jiri chuckled. "Corey told me you'd come after the watch and would probably end up with it. 'Stubborn,' he called you, I well remember. *Stupid*'s a better word for you."

"What good is the watch to you?" Mike demanded. "Why should you go to so much trouble to hunt me down?"

Jiri spat out the answer. "Nobody bests Jiri Logan. Especially a half-growed whippersnapper! I'd be a laughingstock to my friends who heard what Corey said. Some even have a good-size bet riding on the outcome." Anger twisted Jiri's face. "Give me the watch," he demanded.

"It's not yours," Mike insisted.

Jiri took a step forward, and Mike backed against the rail. "It is now."

Jiri suddenly lunged, but Mike ducked, the rope whipping out of his hands. To Mike's horror, Jiri's ankle caught in a twist of the rope, and he lost his balance, the force of his lunge carrying him over the railing.

Mike heard a slap as Jiri hit the water. In shock, Mike leaned over the rail.

Jiri surfaced, his pale face breaking through the waves

set up by the paddlewheel. His mouth opened in a desperate shout, but the boat's engines and the splash of the paddlewheel were so noisy, Mike was unable to hear him. Frozen in terror, he watched Jiri go under, then surface again among the flotsam and driftwood, this time farther from the boat.

He's going to drown! Mike realized. *I can't let him drown!*

"Man overboard!" he screamed. "Help! Man overboard!"

Two of the crew appeared at Mike's side. "Where?" one of them shouted, already preparing a line to throw.

Mike and the two men stared at the muddy water, seeing nothing more than ripples from the paddle.

"He's gone!" Mike whispered. He leaned against the rail, feeling sick. "It's too late. He's gone."

17

JIM, ALONG WITH a few passengers and crew members, ran to the deck to see why Mike had shouted. As one of the crew rushed off to inform the captain, Mike drew Jim aside.

"It was Jiri," he whispered. "He tried to attack me. I ducked, and he lost his balance and went overboard. I called for help, but it was too late. He disappeared in the waves."

Jim put an arm around his friend's shoulders and held him firmly. "Get hold of yourself," he said. "And whatever you do, don't tell who it was or how it happened. If you blurt out the whole story of why Jiri was after you, you'll find yourself escorted off the boat and into a Confederate prison for sure."

Mike couldn't help shivering. "I should have acted faster. I should have tried to save him. No matter how much I hated him, I didn't mean to kill him."

"You didn't kill him. You yelled for help, and you can't be blamed for what happened." As the captain and second mate came striding across the deck, Jim whispered, "Remember, you can't deliver your friend's watch to his sister if you're in prison. First thing off, the guard will snatch it."

Mike gulped. He had *two* pocket watches to deliver, not just one, and Jim was right. What good would it do Jiri or anyone else if Mike blurted out the entire story?

As the boat's officers arrived, the captain immediately assumed authority. "I understand your name is Michael Kelly, and you were hired in Jefferson City as a deckhand."

"Yes, sir," Mike answered. Out of respect, he pulled off his cap and clutched it to his chest.

"You seem to be the only one who saw the incident take place," the captain said. "I'd like to hear your story."

Mike took a deep breath. "I was coiling rope, sir. Someone passed me, and next I heard the splash of water. I saw a head come up out there"—Mike pointed—"and then again there, when he came up a second time. I realized what was happening so I yelled 'Man overboard,' and two of the crew came running."

One of the crew spoke up. "Dooley and I were on hand, Captain, but we didn't see anything. I wondered at the time if the lad could have heard a fish jump and imagined he saw someone. This old river's full of floating logs and who knows what else."

The captain turned to the second mate. "Do a passenger check. Account for every single person. And have one of your personnel do the same with the crew." To Mike he said, not unkindly, "You did the right thing by calling for help, so there's no need to look troubled. For now, I believe you have some work assignments to take care of."

His glance rested briefly on each of the other crew members present, so the group around Mike quickly dispersed. Jim paused just long enough to grip Mike's shoulder and whisper, "Good job. Everything's going to work out just fine. You'll see."

Less than an hour after the accident, Mike was back at

work. While polishing the lamp fittings on the top deck, he tried to sort out his thoughts. *Jiri was a Confederate soldier. If he'd been killed on the battlefield, would I have cared? Not a whit. So why do I feel guilty that he drowned? If Jiri had gotten his hands on me, I might have been the one to go overboard.* It all made sense, yet Mike couldn't ease the heavy feeling in the pit of his stomach. If it weren't for him, Jiri wouldn't be dead.

But as Mike was caught up in the routine of work on the riverboat and soothed by the slow sluggish pace of the giant paddlewheeler, he began to forget his troubles. During the next two days he managed to share a few pleasurable and relaxing moments with Jim. They talked about old times in New York City, friends left behind, and the open spaces of the West—which they'd both come to love.

"I've heard that even farther west there's a range of mountains that reach the sky," Mike said.

Jim grinned. "Better yet, some of those mountains are filled with gold and silver nuggets, just lying there for the taking."

Mike scoffed and poked Jim's shoulder. "If that's so, then why aren't you out there filling bags with nuggets and living like a king?"

Jim laughed. "I'll go there someday," he said, "when my days on the river are over."

"And when will that be?"

"I'll know when it's time."

On the third day, Seth interrupted their talk by hitting the cabin door with his fist and shouting, "We're fixin' to dock soon at Lexington! All hands topside and ready for work."

Mike knew the landing routine by heart, having practiced it when the boat had docked at Booneville and Glasgow. He stood at the prow, port side, clutching a thin line with a monkey ball fastened to one end as a weight. The other end of the line was firmly attached to one of the heavy ropes used to wrap around the cleats on the dock so the boat could be moored.

As the ship approached the dock, Mike expertly twirled the monkey ball, slinging it across to a waiting dockhand, who caught it and began to reel in the mooring line. At the stern of the ship, Jim stood prepared to do the same as soon as the stern began to swing toward the dock.

Mike ran to his next job, helping to lower the long gangplank down and over to the port side. With a bump the boat docked and was securely moored, and the gangplank dropped into place.

For a moment, Mike enjoyed watching some of the passengers depart, but his attention was caught by the crowd on the landing who'd come to see the steamboat's arrival. Two women rushed, open armed, to greet a friend, and before the crowd closed together again, Mike saw a handful of Confederate soldiers standing alone at the back. Some carefully scrutinized the passengers leaving the ship, while others searched the deck.

Mike quickly stepped back. Using the swarm of passengers on ship as a shield, he cut to the starboard side of the boat, where he knew he'd find Jim. "Tell me—you know the river. Could Jiri have made it to shore?" Mike asked.

"Only if he was a good strong swimmer."

Mike glanced over his shoulder. "There's a half-dozen Confederate soldiers on the landing. It's obvious they're searching for someone, and I have a feeling it's me."

"Is Jiri among them?"

"I don't know."

Jim slowly shook his head. "I don't understand. Why does Jiri care so much about that watch?"

"For one thing, he's got a fierce amount of pride," Mike said. "And to make matters worse, there's a bet involved." He brightened. "Still, I feel better, thinking he might be alive. I didn't like to think I was responsible for his death."

"You're a strange one, Mike," Jim said. "If it was me Jiri was after, I'd feel better knowing he was down at the bottom of the old muddy."

"I can't risk staying on the *Mary Belle*, since he might still be looking for me," Mike said. "I'll leave the boat and cut across country to St. Joe."

"I'll go with you," Jim said.

"You can't leave your job."

Jim grinned. "I'll never get around to finding all that gold and silver if I stay on the river. Besides, you'll be safer if you've got someone to travel with."

"What about Seth? How will he fill our jobs?"

"That's no problem. He won't have any trouble finding deckhands here in Lexington."

Mike glanced back at the chattering groups of passengers. "I have to leave now. My only chance to escape is if I can hide among the passengers."

"Then now it is," Jim said. He raced Mike to the cabin, where they snatched up their possessions and headed for the main deck. Mike pulled his cap low over his head as he and Jim elbowed into the middle of the crowd. Mike crept behind a plump woman dressed in full hoopskirts, thankful to find such a good shield from the soldiers.

The woman stopped to greet friends, but Mike was able to keep under the cover of the swarm of passengers. At the first opportunity he scooted into a nearby alley and waited. Sooner or later Jim would find him.

It took only a few minutes. Jim leaned against a wall as he said, "You were right about the Rebs. As they headed toward the gangplank, I heard them saying your name. The minute all the passengers for Lexington have gone ashore, they'll probably board the *Mary Belle*."

"Was Jiri with them?"

"I don't know."

"We need to get away from here," Mike said.

Jim smiled. "Your leg's a lot better, isn't it? You can move much faster now than you could before."

Mike was hopeful. "It's a good thing," he said, "because I figure we've got at least eighty miles or so to travel. It's a long walk to St. Joe."

18

FOLLOWING SHELTERED BACK roads that led them away from the river, Mike and Jim made their way northwest. With the small amount of cash they had between them, they bought meals from farm wives and were granted permission to sleep in haylofts. Because they were too young to be soldiers, no one asked if they were sympathetic to the North or the South. And having left Jiri and his company behind them, the boys felt freed of an enormous burden.

On the third night of their journey, a friendly farmer and his wife, Otto and Maud Nieman, shared a late supper with Mike and Jim in their kitchen.

"Do you have family?" Mrs. Nieman asked kindly.

"Yes," Mike answered.

"Are they near? Or are you far from home?"

"Some are in Kansas, some in and around St. Joe," Mike said politely.

"Good," Mrs. Nieman said. "And what about you, Jim? Have you no one at all?"

"I'm an orphan," Jim told her.

"Dear boy," Mrs. Nieman murmured, and ladled more stew onto Jim's nearly empty plate.

Mike was just mopping up the rich stew broth with a chunk of bread when the kitchen door opened and a husky young man entered.

"Stanley!" Mrs. Nieman cried, and jumped up to hug him.

"We thought you wouldn't be able to take care of your business so soon," Mr. Nieman told him. "We weren't expecting you back from Lexington until Friday."

Lexington! Mike glanced at Jim with alarm.

"Business went well, so I finished early," Stanley answered. He stared at Mike's hair, then took a long slow look at both Mike and Jim.

"Michael Kelly and Jim Riley," Mr. Nieman said. "I'd like you to meet our son, Stanley Nieman."

"Weren't you recently in Lexington?" Stanley asked Mike.

What has Stanley heard? He knows something! From the expression on Jim's face, Mike could tell that Jim felt the same concern.

"Lexington? That's quite a ways from here." Mike faked a yawn. "If you don't mind, Mr. Nieman, we're tired and we'd like to turn in. You said we could sleep in your hayloft?"

"You're welcome to it," Mr. Nieman assured him.

"We'll help you with the dishes first," Mike offered, but Mrs. Nieman laughed and glanced at her son with loving eyes.

"*Nein,*" she said. "We haven't seen Stanley for two weeks, so we have much to talk about. But you boys come in for breakfast before you leave in the morning. Some biscuits and eggs will give you a good start to the day."

Mike and Jim thanked the Niemans, picked up their knapsacks and bedrolls, and left through the kitchen door.

The moment they were outside, Mike held a finger to his lips and crept under the open kitchen window.

"You're harboring thieves!" Stanley was saying. "The one with red hair—he not only stole a fine pocket watch from a Confederate soldier, he physically attacked him and broke his leg."

Jim sucked in his breath and shot Mike a glance.

"How could he do that? He's just a boy," Mrs. Nieman complained.

"He's a Union soldier, escaped when he was captured."

"No! He's not old enough to be a soldier. I can't believe that story."

"Ma," Stanley persisted, "I heard it from the Confederate soldier himself. He's offering a reward, and I'm going to claim it."

"Stanley!" Mr. Nieman demanded. "What are you doing with my rifle?"

"I'm going after that pair," Stanley answered. "I'll tie them up and take them back to Lexington. I told you, Pa, I plan on collecting that reward."

"Listen to me, Stanley—" Mr. Nieman began, but Mike and Jim didn't wait to hear the rest. Swinging their knapsacks and bedrolls up on their backs, they ran toward the road that led into the woods.

A shot whizzed by Mike's ear.

Jim put on a burst of speed, yelling over his shoulder, "Hurry, Mike! Faster!"

Another shot! A shell slammed into the dust near Mike's feet, and he ran with all his strength, wincing at the sharp pain in his leg.

"Stanley, stop!" Mike heard Mrs. Nieman scream.

Then, "Ma! Leave me alone!"

Mike and Jim cut into the shelter of the woods, running and hobbling without a stop until they were nearly a mile north of the Niemans' farm. Mike, his chest heaving as he tried to catch his breath, threw himself down on the ground. Jim flopped beside him.

"Poor old Jiri broke his leg," Jim said, and Mike could hear the satisfaction in his words. "Jiri may want the watch, but it looks like he wants *you* even more."

Mike remembered the aftermath of Wilson's Creek, when Jiri told Corey to shoot him. He shuddered. "When we reach St. Joe, we'll be safe," he told Jim.

Jim stood up and stretched. "Then let's get started," he answered. "No sleep for us tonight. We'd better keep traveling."

For two days they kept to the road, ready to leap into ditches or cornfields or woods at the first sound of horses' hooves. At last, just before noon they straggled into the town of St. Joseph. Mike was never so glad to see the familiar bustle—shoppers, trappers, families gathering supplies for treks west, businessmen in high starched collars and top hats, riverboat men, and a few children, who sometimes darted dangerously close to the horses and lumbering wagon wheels.

The town was much as it had been when Mike arrived on an orphan train, and his heart began to ache as memories rose like ghosts to taunt him. But at least Ma lived here now, and his friends Katherine Banks and Andrew MacNair. He smiled at the sight of Katherine's store.

"Wake up, Mike," Jim said. "Tell me where we're headed now. Your ma's house? With that reward on your head, it's better that not many people know we're here."

More than anything he could think of, Mike wanted to see his mother, but he shook his head. "First I'll take Billy Whitley's pocket watch to his wife, Aggie. Then I can relax." He scratched his chest and smiled. "And have what I've been longing for—a hot bath."

At that moment the door to Katherine Banks's store

opened, and Katherine stepped out onto the wooden sidewalk with a customer.

"Mrs. Banks!" Mike shouted.

She turned, shading her eyes against the sun, and smiled as she recognized him. "Mike Kelly!"

Mike hurried to join her and introduced Jim.

"Have you seen your mother yet?" Katherine asked. "I know she's been expecting you."

"Not yet," Mike said.

Katherine caught hold of a boy who came scampering past. "Johnny," she said, "run and fetch Mrs. Noreen Murphy. Tell her Mike's here. There'll be a peppermint stick for you when you get back."

"And Mrs. Billy Whitley," Mike told him, pressing one of his few remaining coins into the boy's hand. "She's staying with relations on Chester Street. Do you know her? I'm carrying a parcel to her from her husband."

"I know Mrs. Whitley," Katherine said, and she gave Johnny directions to the house.

The boy took off in a hurry, and Katherine turned to Mike. "We've heard so much about you, Mike. Tell me—"

But Katherine was elbowed aside by the scowling banker, Mr. Crandon, who was even plumper and pastier than Mike remembered him.

"Someone call the sheriff!" Mr. Crandon sputtered. "Mike Kelly should be under arrest!"

Before Mike could speak, Stanley Nieman stepped around from behind Mr. Crandon. "We don't need the sheriff. He's *my* prisoner."

Terrified, Mike stammered, "I'm nobody's prisoner! I haven't done anything wrong!"

"You're a thief!" Mr. Crandon shouted. "Stole a Confederate soldier's watch!"

A crowd had begun to gather, and Mike could hear mutterings. "What'd he say about the Confederates?"

"My son's with Price's Missouri State Guard," said a man in the crowd.

"This boy's done something to a Confederate soldier," said another.

"Then he ought to be in jail."

Mr. Crandon suddenly reached out and snatched Mike's knapsack, ripping it from his shoulders. "We'll prove you're lying!" he yelled at Mike. "If you stole the watch, it will be in here!"

To Mike's horror, Mr. Crandon pulled Billy Whitley's watch from its envelope, the papers with it scattering on the ground. "Here! What's this? A second watch?" Mr. Crandon cried, and came up with Todd's watch.

"I can explain!" Mike yelled at him.

As Mr. Crandon upended Mike's knapsack, Mike's Union Army uniform dropped to his feet.

"Look at that uniform! He's a Union spy!" someone shouted.

Stanley reached for the watches, but Mr. Crandon, who looked as if he were trying to appraise their value, quickly moved them out of his reach.

The man who'd said his son was with Price's Missouri Guard spoke up. "We know how the armies handle spies! They're hanged on the spot!"

"Especially Union spies!" someone chimed in, and grabbed Mike's arms from behind.

"No!" Katherine shouted.

Mike saw his mother trying desperately to elbow her way through the rapidly growing crowd.

Stanley made another swipe toward the watches, but Mr. Crandon held them high. "I'll take care of these watches," he said.

"Not mine, you won't!"

A plump woman, her bonnet askew, stepped up on the edge of a horse trough and clung to a lamppost for balance.

"All of you be quiet!" she shouted at the crowd. "I have something to say!"

The angry people on the street turned toward her in stunned silence. The woman cleared her throat, tried to adjust her bonnet with one hand, and said more calmly, "For those I haven't met as yet, my name is Aggie Whitley. My husband, Billy Whitley, is with the Second Kansas Infantry, where this boy—Mike Kelly—served as a drummer until he was wounded at Wilson's Creek. When Mike Kelly was discharged, my husband Billy asked him to deliver his watch to me. He wrote and told me to expect Mike." She pointed. "That gold one with the design etched into it—that's my watch."

Mike spoke up. "The letters Billy sent with it are on the ground where Mr. Crandon dropped them."

Mrs. Whitley drew herself up haughtily and stared down her nose at Mr. Crandon. "I'll thank you to pick them up and give them to me, along with my watch."

Mr. Crandon, huffing a bit, did as she had told him. Then he said triumphantly, "This other watch, though—this was taken from one of our boys fighting bravely for the South."

"No, it wasn't," Mike said.

The crowd began to mutter and bicker, but Mrs. Whitley, who had a fine pair of lungs to Mike's way of thinking, shouted them down. "You heard me out and found that Mr. Crandon was wrong. Now give the boy a chance. Listen to what he has to say!"

Mike tugged free of the arms that held him. He was frightened at the sight of the faces turned toward him, many of them tight with anger, but he took a deep breath and began. "The watch Mr. Crandon's holding belongs to a friend of mine, Todd Blakely," he began. He told the crowd about how Todd had made Mike promise to take the watch to Emily, his sister; about lying wounded in a hollow after the battle was over; and about how Corey had chided Jiri Logan for robbing the dead.

"War's a horror you can't believe unless you're in it with guns blasting around you and wounded men screaming in pain," Mike said. "I saw a Confederate soldier shoot a Union soldier, then hold him in his arms while he cried, 'I shot my pa! God help me, I shot my pa!' "

Mike heard gasps of horror. Nearby a woman whimpered, thrusting a handkerchief to her mouth.

"And it's not just soldiers who live in nightmares. I met a woman whose secessionist husband informs on Union sympathizers, then rides at night with patrols who burn their barns and houses. People are doing evil things to each other —all because of the war."

The crowd was shocked into silence. No one moved as Mike continued. "I tried to serve my country the best way I knew how, and I did until I was shot in battle. If the war goes on for the next few years, I'll enlist again—this time as a soldier. But I'm not a spy, and I'll never be one."

Some of the people in the crowd turned and walked away. Mr. Crandon still held Todd's watch, but he didn't resist as Katherine opened his fingers. The watch in her hand, she said to Stanley Nieman, "Go back where you came from. You'll find no support here."

Ma rushed toward Mike with a hug that nearly knocked him off his feet. "Oh, Michael, Michael, I'm so proud of you!" she cried. She held Mike at arm's length, searching his face while tears trickled into her smile. "You'll stay with me until you're well again," she said.

"I'll stay for just a little while, Ma," he told her. "I want to spend some time with you and Peg and visit Danny, but then I need to get back to Fort Leavenworth. Louisa is expecting me—and Todd's sister Emily."

For just an instant disappointment clouded Ma's face, but she covered it with a smile. "You seem so much older, Mike. You've grown."

"I still have a bit of growing to do," Mike said as she

hugged him again. "You might say three inches and three years to go."

"If you're talking about reenlisting—"

"Ma," Mike told her, "if you're going to ask me to promise I'll wait until I'm legally old enough, well, I've already made that promise to myself."

As his mother wrapped him in her arms again, Mike laughed. "Let's forget about war for a while," he said, "and go find Peg."

A week later Mike rode the ferry across the river with Jim. "I'll soon be off for the mountains and the gold and silver hidden within them," Jim said, stroking the horse he'd bought for his journey—a horse that was slightly sway-backed but had sound teeth. "I wish you'd come with me, Mike."

At the moment Mike wished he could go, too. Jim's offer was certainly tempting. But he answered, "I've got to keep my promise to Todd and the promise I made to myself."

"Good luck," Jim said, and Mike counted on that wish as he traveled south to Fort Leavenworth.

As Mike entered the fort, a strong hand gripped his shoulder. "We heard some of what you did, lad," Sergeant Duncan bellowed, "and we're hopin' to hear the rest."

"Later," Mike said, pulling away. There'd be time for war stories later. "I need to tell Lou—my mother that I'm home again."

Louisa affectionately folded Mike in her arms, tearfully scolding and praising him. "No more running away," she said. "Promise me, Mike."

"I promise," he answered. No need at the moment to tell her his plans to reenlist when he reached the age of sixteen.

Mike took a deep breath and faced the inevitable. "I have to see Emily Blakely. I've brought her Todd's watch."

Louisa wiped her eyes and pulled on her bonnet, tying it

firmly under her chin. "And Mrs. Blakely," she said. "We'll call on them together."

Mike protested, "There's no need for you to go."

But Louisa opened the door, waiting for Mike to follow her. "This will be a difficult time for you," she said, "and I think it will help you to know that your mother is there by your side."

As Mike had guessed, Mrs. Blakely had many questions to ask about Todd. Mike couldn't hold back his own tears as Mrs. Blakely burst into sobs.

"I—I'm sorry, Mrs. Blakely," Mike murmured. "Sorrier than anyone could know."

"I'm not blaming you for what happened, Michael," Mrs. Blakely told him, wiping away her tears. "Todd always had a mind of his own."

Emily broke in. "He talked about going off to war afore you even came here."

"He wanted to be like his father, the captain," Mike began, but he couldn't go on. He wanted badly to know if Captain Blakely had survived the Battle of Bull Run, but he was terrified to ask.

With a soggy handkerchief Mrs. Blakely rubbed hard at her reddened nose. "That's *Major* Blakely now," she said. "My husband received a field promotion."

If only Todd had known his father had survived the battle with honor. If only Todd could be with his family now. Mike fished into his pocket and brought forth Todd's watch, placing it in Emily's hand. "This meant more to Todd than anything else he ever owned," he said, "and he asked me to bring this to you, Emily."

"Thank you," Emily whispered. Tears ran down her cheeks as she held the watch to her lips.

One promise fulfilled, one to go, Mike thought. But the promise to himself would take three years to come about. Right now he was glad to be home.

* * *

Jennifer sighed as Grandma closed Frances Mary's journal. "I learned in history class that the Civil War lasted four years," she said. "Did Mike do what he'd planned and become a soldier?"

"All the Kellys were involved in the war, in one way or another," Grandma answered. "As Mike said, the war reached everyone. It changed every life, and innocent people often suffered greatly in their attempts to help the cause in which they believed. Think how terrible it must have been for the Kellys when one of them was arrested for being a Union spy!"

Jeff sat bolt upright. "Mike was arrested? But he said he'd never be a spy!"

"Mike wasn't the spy," Grandma said. She stood and asked, "I've got to run some errands in town. Would you like to go with me?"

Jennifer jumped to her feet. "Grandma!" she complained. "I can't stand it! You have to tell us which Kelly became a spy!"

"I will," Grandma said, and broke into a grin. "But not until tomorrow morning."

"I may not last until then," Jennifer moaned.

"You will if you want to hear a truly unusual story," Grandma said. "Tomorrow we'll read the journal again—I promise."

About the Author

Joan Lowery Nixon is the author of more than a hundred books for young readers. She has served as regional vice-president for the Southwest Chapter of the Mystery Writers of America and is the only four-time winner of the Edgar Allan Poe Best Juvenile Mystery Award given by that society. She is also a two-time winner of the Western Writers of America's Golden Spur Award, which she won for *A Family Apart* and *In the Face of Danger,* the first and third books of the Orphan Train Adventures. She was moved by the true experiences of the children on the nineteenth-century orphan trains to research and write the Orphan Train Adventures, which also include *Caught in the Act, A Place to Belong,* and *Keeping Secrets.*

Joan Lowery Nixon and her husband live in Houston.

Maggie